IT'S ALWAYS BEEN YOU

A Valentines Friends-to-Lovers, Best Friend's Brother Romance

M.M. Wakeford

Praise for It's Always Been You:

"A lovely and heartwarming romance that sweetened my evening. I love a good contemporary romance novella and this one certainly hit all the good spots... I devoured this book whole and could not put it down." Lilith - Goodreads review

"OH WOW this was a great story. It was a page turner and the suspense was sweet... I was on the edge of my seat and I couldn't even put it down. The chemistry was captivating." Trina - Goodreads review

"This was a short read, and yet beautifully written. It felt like witnessing a love story of two people who met in their prime, and seeing them fall deeper in love as they grow old together." NiqueReads - Goodreads review

"I thought this was a super cute short read for Valentines Day. The writing was great and it was such a heartwarming story." Courtney - Goodreads review

"A very sweet, wholesome valentines novella with a sprinkle of spice!" Kirsty - Goodreads review

"This is exactly what it says: a sweet, heartwarming valentine romance." Leslie - Goodreads review

"A sweet love story set in London, it follows our FMC through flash backs and present day. If you're looking for a quick sweet read for Valentine's Day, add this one to your list!" Roberta - Goodreads review

"A quick easy read that I enjoyed from the start." Noreen - Goodreads review

"A short but captivating novel that captivates with its simplicity. The writing is direct and effective, delivering a story that, although brief, keeps you hooked. A great

story for those who like short books that are easy to read in one sitting.” Lia - Goodreads review

“This was a cute novella perfect for a Valentine’s Day read! I liked how the timeline was structured and the dual POV for the start of their relationship. Part of me wishes it had been longer, but I liked how much feeling and plot the author worked in at less than 100 pages!” Heather - Goodreads review

“Highly recommend this one if you want a little bit of spice and a super cute dual pov over multiple timelines in your quick read.” Sam - Goodreads review

“What a sweet little Valentine’s Day novella. This is a cute winter read... Wilfred is so sweet and such a gentleman. Karima’s marble cake recipe at the end was such a sweet touch!” Nycole - Goodreads review

“I really enjoyed this heartwarming Valentine's Day romance... If you like romantic, quick reads about mature couples who still are very much in love after decades of marriage, you are sure to enjoy this book!” Marion - Goodreads review

“Well written, fast paced valentine novella. Full of drama, friendship, love and a changing timeline.” Rose - Goodreads review

Dedication

To A, my own real-life Valentine. This book may be a work of fiction, but the spirit of our story is in every page. Thank you for being my rock, my biggest advocate and my best friend.

Preface

While this is a work of fiction, this story also contains autobiographical elements. It's a distillation of my own personal history as an immigrant from the Middle East growing up in the UK, feeling like I didn't fit in. It's also a version of my own love story with the wonderful man I am privileged to call husband to this day, seventeen plus years after we first became a couple.

Though I have changed details here and there to keep this a fictional account, at its heart, this is my story, and thus the most personal work I have published so far. To those that may claim the main character, Karima, does not behave as a Muslim would, I would simply say this. People cannot be typecast—and there is nothing more authentic than telling a story based on one's own life experience.

And yes, he did propose on Valentine's Day...

PART ONE: KARIMA

Chapter 1

A gloomy morning in London

Present day

The soft chime of the alarm clock on the bedside table woke her from a deep sleep. It was going to take a monumental effort to rouse as every instinct she possessed urged her to sink back under the comfortable nest of the duvet tucked around her. She managed to lift sticky eyelids a fraction to see the numbers on the dial— 06:25. Around her, the dark shadows of the room were barely illuminated by the glow of the hallway light which she kept on at night. She closed her eyes again, whispering to herself, "Five more minutes."

February, with its short, gloomy days, was never her favourite month of the year. Oftentimes, she wished she could hibernate the winter away and only wake once the first buds of May were blossoming on the cherry tree outside her house. Wouldn't that be heavenly. She let herself slip back into happy reverie for a few blessed minutes. But not for too long. Duty called.

With a sigh, she threw off the duvet, shivering under the cold air seeping into her warm lair. Gritting her teeth, she brought her legs to the side, finding her slippers, and got to her feet, the muscles in her back creaking painfully with the effort. "This body is not getting any younger," she thought ruefully. She would be fifty next birthday, which was only a few months around the corner. Where had all the years gone by? Rationally, of course, she knew. She could list all the wonderful, trying and everything-in-between things that she had experienced over the last two decades, even though it felt at times as if they had gone by in a flash.

With a deep breath, she forced herself to walk briskly to the bathroom. Some minutes later, washed and dressed, a smattering of light make-up on her face, hair neatly brushed, she made her way down the stairs to the kitchen, inhaling the aroma of coffee freshly brewed in the machine she had programmed the night before. She poured herself a cup, added a dash of milk, then took a grateful sip, beginning to feel much more herself. Nothing could beat that first hit of coffee in the morning. Reaching over the kitchen counter, she grabbed her phone, unhooking it from the charger. It was late night in LA, so there was a chance perhaps that Wilfred might have sent a message.

Eagerness turned to disappointment at the blank screen on her phone. Oh well. It was just a day, like any other. There was no obligation to fall under the spell of the marketing gimmicks and the aisles in the shops heaving with heart-shaped offerings. She had no need for any of them, not when she had the real deal—nearly twenty years of a happy marriage under her belt, thank you very much.

She set about making her sandwich and packing it neatly into her lunch bag, together with an easy peeler and a small packaged muffin, in case she felt the need for something sweet later in the day. As she poured water into her bottle and put fresh slices of bread into the toaster, she chased away the little demon whispering in her ear that it would have been very nice indeed for her dear, beloved husband to have done something, anything, to mark the occasion. Perhaps he still might; the day was young after all. Nevertheless, she frowned, deep in thought as she buttered her toast and took it to the table. Had they gotten so comfortable in their relationship as to take each other for granted? Well, in a way they had, and that was not entirely a bad thing. It was good to be sure of your partner, to know without a doubt that you would be together for the long haul, rain or shine.

And yet... and yet. She knew the reasons for her insecurities today. It was Valentine's Day, and for the first time in twenty years, Wilfred and her were apart. Work had necessitated it—in Wilfred's case, the pressures of a big-budget Hollywood movie he was producing, and in hers, the never ending duties that came with being a teacher and senior leader at her school. Only one more day and it would be half-term, but until then, she wasn't free to fly off to LA, much as she would have liked to get away from the cold drabness of London at this time of the year.

It was a miracle, come to think of it, that this situation had never cropped up before. Wilfred had always managed his schedule to ensure he was here for his family on the big days, even though his work involved a great deal of travel back and forth across the pond. They had talked once of moving to California, lock, stock and barrel, but had in the end decided against it. London was their home, the place where they had roots and family, where they wanted their children educated.

The compromise was the frequent travel, though Wilfred did not always go on his own. She joined him whenever school holidays allowed it, and they had become skilful at managing their schedules just right so that their time apart was minimised. It had worked. In every way that mattered, they were a successful partnership. So, she had no reason to feel glum this morning. Looking out the window at the still dark sky, she thought it was probably just a case of Seasonal Affective Disorder, added to which, she missed Wilfred. It had been ten long days since he had left for LA. He had promised to be back on Sunday, after which they would both hopefully have a clear schedule to spend quality time together.

Until then, there was work to be done. Once she had rinsed and put her plate away in the dishwasher, she ran upstairs and knocked on Hamid's bedroom door. "Seven o'clock," she called and received a grunt in response. She stayed a while to make sure her teenage son had got out of bed, starting back down the stairs as he emerged sleepily from his room. "I'm off now," she said. "Love you." He gave an incoherent growl. With a smile, she fetched her coat, checked her bag to make sure she had everything she needed and headed out to work.

Her musings, however, followed her into the car and the half-hour drive to the school where she worked. Who would have thought it, her and Wilfred still together after all these years? They had seemed such an improbable pairing at the start. They came from opposite sides of the social order, with different cultural and religious backgrounds, she a schoolteacher and him a movie producer. A future together had not seemed on the cards for them, not until one fateful encounter changed everything.

20 years previously

Chapter 2

God, that was embarrassing!

Christmas Eve

This really is the last time I do it. At least that's what I tell myself. Just because I've been doing it every year since I turned twenty does not mean the thing is set in stone. It's been very kind of Allegra's family to include me in their Christmas celebrations each year. They mean well—they are super-kind people—but nothing can quite erase the feeling of being a charity case, the poor girl who has nobody to be with at Christmas.

It's not that I'm entirely without family. I'm close to my brother Amir, despite the ten-year age gap. Only thing is, Amir, his wife Ania and their three kids always do Christmas in Ania's native Poland. I have cousins scattered here and there around the world, and several more eking out a living in Kabul, where my family is originally from, but in London, at Christmas, it's only me. I don't mind. Well, not much at any rate.

I've known the Barton-Brownes (the Browne part spelt with an e) ever since Allegra befriended me, the bursary kid at the independent girls' school we both attended in west London. Allegra could have befriended anyone, and to be sure, she did have a large group of acolytes who hung on her every word, but for some bizarre, unknown reason, she chose me. I say this not out of undue modesty. I've got a decent brain in my head—enough at least to have won a free tuition scholarship at a highly selective school—and a dry sense of humour (so dry sometimes that it might require a little watering to become apparent). I'm generally kind—not a Mother Teresa—but I suppose I don't go out of my way to be mean to others. I like indie bands and indie cinema, and I have a secret addiction to Marvel comic books. What I'm trying to say in a roundabout way is that I'm not boring or inconsequential. There is no earthly reason why anyone would not want to befriend me. But here's the rub. Allegra is not just anyone.

If anyone was born under a lucky star, it was Allegra Barton-Browne. Blessed with a tall, sylph-like figure and with the face of an English rose, she was the girl that miraculously went through her teens without a single blemish on her perfectly rosy complexion. Along with the good looks was a bright smile that shone like a beacon, drawing people to her effortlessly. It was the smile of a person that was happy, mischievous and in great charity with the world. And why should she not be? Great was her privilege to grow up in a beautiful mansion overlooking the River Thames basking in the affection of her generous, easy-going parents. And if that was not all, on top of these wondrous advantages was the fact that Allegra was talented. She was clever too, earning straight As in her A Levels and GCSEs, but it was at art that she excelled. No surprise then that her destination post-school was Oxford University, to study for an art degree.

So, when I said that Allegra's befriending of me was a bizarre occurrence, I hope this additional context helps to explain what I meant. I was in Year 8 when this overture of friendship was bestowed on me. I had spent my first year of secondary school hiding in corners, quiet as a church mouse, not knowing how to fit in with the other girls, most of whom had known each other since prep school. There was only one other bursary girl in my year group, Veronica, a nerdish swot with greasy-looking hair who seemed happy to spend every spare minute with her face buried in a book. Of course, I have no objection to books. I am rather fond of them myself. Only, it meant that Veronica was a bit of a non-starter when it came to my finding a kindred spirit to hang out with. So it was that I spent that first year alone and quite miserable, until that is, Allegra 'discovered' me.

It's no understatement to say that she lifted me out of obscurity. Almost overnight, invites to parties and other social dos began to come my way. The friendship itself blossomed while we were rehearsing for our Year 8 play. It was a long-standing tradition at the school for Year 8s to perform three one-act plays, each written and directed by the seniors in the sixth form. It just happened that I was chosen for a part in the same play that Allegra was in. I have no recollection now what the play was about, only that my part was that of a gangster. I had one line I had to utter, in a mean and menacing voice. As luck would have it, each time my turn came to say this one line, I was attacked by the worst case of stage fright which manifested itself in an uncontrollable fit of giggles.

The sixth formers in charge of directing our play were frustrated and annoyed. Despite all their helpful stage directions, the same thing occurred every time—a mad fit of giggles. Then Allegra went to whisper something in their ear. Shortly afterwards, I was approached by one of the sixth formers. "Karima," she said, "we think you might be a better fit for another part. How about a swap with Allegra? She can take on the role of Steve while you play Millie." Millie was the sweet and loved-up girlfriend of one of the other side characters, and not much was demanded of her except to deliver two words with a smile (and maybe also now with a giggle). The deal was gratefully accepted. Allegra acquitted herself well in the role of Steve, and I managed not to inflict too much damage to the production in my part as a giggling Millie.

During a lull in the rehearsing, I found myself next to Allegra, and feeling tongue-tied, forced out some words of gratitude. She smiled her beatific smile. "No probs," she said. "As long as you don't mind my swapping you for a smaller part."

"Of course not!" I protested.

"Cool." She observed me curiously. "So, Karima Afzal, tell me about yourself. Where are you from originally?"

Ok, so not a very PC question to ask, but to be fair, with a name like mine, it was obvious that I was from a family of immigrants. I replied, "My parents are from Kabul—you know, in Afghanistan."

Her mouth formed a round O. "How super interesting!" she exclaimed, then enquired, "When was it you came to England?"

"I was very young, around five years old," I shrugged.

She nodded emphatically. "Right." Then, brow wrinkling, "Was it the war?"

"The war?"

"The reason your family came here," she clarified. "The war that's going on there with the Russians and the Mujahideen rebels. I've heard about it on the news."

"Oh," I said stupidly. "Yes it was." At her expectant look, I explained further. "When the Russians invaded Afghanistan, there was a huge uprising in Kabul and lots of people were killed. My mum and dad decided, along with many others, that it was best to flee the country."

"It must have been dreadful!" she shuddered dramatically in a way that I could never hope to emulate.

Then she probed some more. "So, you arrived here as refugees?"

"Yes," I explained patiently. "First, we went to Pakistan and spent some years in a refugee camp there. And then we were lucky enough to be brought over to the UK through the work of a charity."

"I suppose that was lucky," she said. "Can't have been easy though."

"As dad tells it, those first few years after we left Kabul were the pits of hell, but he likes to exaggerate. I was too young to remember."

She continued to regard me as if I was the most fascinating person she had ever met. "Karima," she said. "Fancy coming over to my place Friday after school? We can watch a movie on DVD or something."

"Your place?" I repeated dumbly.

She smiled encouragingly.

"Err, yes, that would be nice, thanks," I replied.

Her place turned out to be a huge mansion on the exclusive Chiswick Mall with gardens that went all the way down to the river's edge. It was immediately apparent, more so than at school, that Allegra's world and mine were miles apart. I met her parents, who invited me to dinner. That too was an experience quite different to the casually chaotic meals we had at home. Our way at my place was to dump the food in a serving dish on the table, and everyone helped themselves noisily. Not so in the Barton-Browne household. Meticulously measured portions were served (on heated plates) then brought to the shabbily elegant dining room. Although a second helping was graciously offered, it was most often declined. No wonder they were all skinny.

Then there was the wine—of good vintage of course. It was ceremoniously uncorked, after which Hugo Barton-

Browne swished it in his glass and took a taste. Only once it met his approval was it then decanted into wine glasses for the adults' delectation. There were separate tumblers for water and a side plate for the bread roll. A delicate portion of pudding followed the main course, then cheese and liqueurs. With the knowledge of adulthood, I can see this was nothing less than a restaurant experience at home, though to a young girl of twelve, it seemed foreign. More accurately, it made *me* feel like the foreigner, for they all appeared to be wonderfully at home with such practices.

I'm not sure what prompted that first invitation to Allegra's home. A desire to do a good deed for the refugee bursary girl? A curiosity about my otherness? No idea. We hit it off that first time though, and one invitation led to another. I reciprocated with invites to dinner at my house. I can only imagine how exotic that must have seemed to Allegra, though she bore it well with her customary bright smile and managed to charm mum, dad and even my brother.

For the first few months of this new existence as Allegra's official best friend, I pinched myself and waited for my brief moment in the limelight to end. It didn't. Our friendship endured over the years, despite our manifest differences. I have at times of introspection wondered about it and come to the conclusion that we each complement something in the other. Her bright affability brings me out of my shell and softens my sharp edges. My quiet constancy gives Allegra a security in our friendship which I don't think she easily finds in her circle of other friends. I don't gossip, and Allegra knows she can confide in me without any word of it reaching other ears; like the time she told me about having a threesome with her then boyfriend and another bloke, a college friend from Oxford. The way she told it, the experience was mind blowing, but she broke up with that boyfriend shortly afterwards, so one could say the experience was also relationship blowing.

There's another factor too, which I was slow to notice at first. Her family, while kind and generous, always addressing each other as 'darling', were not of the physically demonstrative sort. Put that in sharp contrast with mine, who were always hugging and openly showing our affection. Sitting of an evening in front of the telly, mum would braid my hair or stroke my arm gently. There was always a cuddle to be had at her ample bosom. In the comfort of her arms, I would breathe in her familiar scent, a mixture of spices from cooking at the stove and the incense she liked to air the rooms with. Dad too always had a smile and a hug for me. I liked nothing better than to drape my arms around him and stroke the fuzzy stubble on his cheeks while he teased me about something or the other. I never had any doubt of their love for me, though we almost never expressed it verbally with 'I love you'. I can see now that for Allegra, it must have been a novel and welcome sensation to be in our midst.

There is one more thing Allegra and I have in common. We both are one of two siblings with a much older brother. Wilfred Barton-Browne is seven years her senior, and the product of her mum's previous relationship. He was subsequently adopted by Hugo and took on the family name. Tall and athletic, Wilfred is another Barton-Browne blessed with looks, talent and success. I didn't see much of him those first few years of my friendship with Allegra, as he was away at Oxford, then sharing a London flat with some friends, after which he was off to live in America for a few years. He's now a big name movie producer. That Emmy-winning adaptation of *Shadow of the Moon*, one of my all-time fave novels—that was produced by him.

I still don't run into him that often. He's there, of course, at birthdays and Christmas, the occasional Sunday lunch too. I've had a crush on Wilfred ever since I first met him. I don't keep many secrets from Allegra, but for this one. The crush, to my shame, has not abated, even now at age twenty-nine. In direct proportion to the strength of my crush has been the imperative to hide its existence from everyone I know. I am never the most talkative of people, but in Wilfred's presence, I become even meeker, responding to enquiries but not initiating any conversation of my own. He treats me with casual friendliness, nothing more. I'm sure I'm just an afterthought where he's concerned.

I've observed from afar, on the Internet and through titbits of conversation from Allegra, as he's dated a series of beautiful women—models, actresses, society girls, basically everything that I'm not. He had a girlfriend for a few years whom he lived with when he was in America, but that relationship foundered after his return to the UK. Since then, it's been a string of casual girlfriends, the common denominator being the high attractiveness factor of each girl. Who could blame him? When you have the world at your feet, you can afford to pick and choose the best. All that to say, I'm not foolish enough to harbour any ambitions where he's concerned. I'm not hiding under a bushel, waiting for him to discover me. Most days, I don't even think of him—our lives are too far apart. It's just that on the occasions when I do happen to encounter him, my heart pitter-patters at double speed, and I'm unbearably conscious of his presence. After that, it takes a couple of days, or weeks, to flush him out of my system and get back to an even footing.

Having said that, there have been two occasions when I've felt more than momentary attention from Wilfred, both times when I've experienced a loss. When mum died of breast cancer, I was just fourteen, and he was at the time living in America. He must have obtained my home address from Allegra, for a sweetly worded letter arrived from him a week later. I still have it, hidden safe in a box of precious knick-knacks. Then, in my third year at university, dad keeled over from a heart attack. The day of the funeral, I got a text message from Wilfred.

Unknown number: May your dad rest in peace, Karima. Call me if you ever need anything. Wilfred x

I saved the number on my phone as WBB. Needless to say, I never did call. It was a kind sentiment, and I suppose if ever I were in a desperate situation, it might be a lifeline to have Wilfred on speed dial. But though it's been hard, losing parents I loved, there's never been any other choice but to carry on. I've been alright. I got through university, dabbled at a few jobs then trained as a teacher. I've even dated (a little bit and mostly unsatisfactorily).

Losing mum and dad made me and Amir close though. When I bought my own place not long ago, a small ex-council house on Sundew Avenue, in the unfashionable part of Shepherds Bush just off the Westway, I chose a location that was an easy distance from Amir's house. I'm often at his place, and I'm very involved with my nieces and nephew. It helps also that I get on well with Ania, who is the most easy-going and big-hearted person I know. So, I've been doing okay. No, really, I have. No one should be sobbing over me.

Which brings me back to the matter of Christmas. Ever since I lost dad, I've had a standing invitation to join the Barton-Brownes both on Christmas Eve and for Christmas lunch. I appreciate the gesture, but nine years on, I'm beginning to feel like it might be time to cut that particular cord. When Allegra called last week right in the middle of a busy lunch break where I was trying to simultaneously eat a sandwich at my desk, mark English books and nominate one of my students for star of the term, I happened to mention that perhaps this year, I might have other plans for Christmas. After a stunned silence, she bit out, "What other plans?"

"I don't know," I mumbled, chowing on my cheese sandwich. "Maybe get a last minute deal on a short break to somewhere warm. Tunisia? Canary Islands?"

"We're all expecting you to join us," she said plaintively, then added, "Your presents are already under the tree."

"I can't keep coming over every year," I said with a sigh. "Eventually, I'll wear out my welcome."

"That is the stupidest thing I've ever heard you say, K," she said, her tone severe. "You're family."

"Actually, I'm not," I said gently.

She scoffed at that. "As good as. Listen, you can go on your short break another time. I might even be tempted to join you—not to the Canaries though. But I'm laying down the law here. At Christmas, your place is with your sister from another mother."

I grimaced. These wrongly worded Americanisms sounded cringe when they came out of her English rose of a mouth. Just then, I spotted a run-on sentence in the book I was marking and circled it with my pink pen. At the same time, I said wearily, "You're not going to take no for an answer, are you?"

"Nope."

"Ok then, but I'm serving you notice that next year, I'll be off somewhere hot. And I'll make sure to book it nice and early so you can't pressgang me into coming over."

"Yeah, yeah," she grumbled, though I knew she was pleased at her little victory. "We'll see about that."

And so, here I am today, drawing up at the gated entrance to the Barton-Browne house in my beat-up Ford Fiesta. The sight of that grand mansion never fails to impress. The contrast between this grandeur and my own little nook of a house is such that I can never be blasé about being here. There's excitement, a touch of trepidation, and of course, awe that I get to spend time in this place that is so out of my reach. Over and above all that though, is a feeling that I don't belong here and never will.

After I'm buzzed into the forecourt, I drive slowly over the gravel to park my car to one side, next to Allegra's smart Mini. I reach over for my overnight bag, then step out, the white pebbles crunching under my feet as I make my way to the front entrance. I barely have time to ring the bell before the door is wrenched open and a grinning Allegra pulls me inside.

"Good," she says, "you're just in time. Let's go for a swim." Of course, the Barton-Browne mansion has a heated indoor pool—and an outdoor one for that matter. But I have not come with the intention of swimming.

I resist the pull of her hand on my arm, shaking my head as I say, "Nooo, Allegra! I haven't even brought a swimsuit."

"Pff," she responds, puffing out the sound through closed lips. "You can borrow one of mine," and she heads off in the direction of the pool house, throwing over her shoulder, "Come on, K, no dawdling." With a sigh, I follow her, my bag slung over one shoulder, silently bemoaning the fact that no swimsuit of Allegra's is likely to fit well over my much more rounded body. At least there won't be an audience to my embarrassment. The pool house, accessed via a long, covered walkway, is very private. So private, in fact, that once upon a time, Allegra and I swam there without a stitch of clothing, daring each other to 'skinny dip'. In retrospect, it was not much of a dare, seeing as there was nobody else but us around, though this did not detract from the frisson we experienced from doing something a little naughty. That was years ago though, when we were both in our teens.

We reach the pool house, entering its muggy atmosphere and going through to the changing room. There, Allegra roots inside a large wooden crate, pulling out a bright pink bikini. "This should do," she says decisively, throwing it in my direction. I catch it doubtfully, eyeing the small scraps of material. She ignores the frown on my face and turns to take out her own swimsuit, a pale yellow bikini with black polka dots. Chatting companionably, we change into our swimwear, going into adjacent cubicles. I might be nervous and out of my element in this house, but I'm easy in Allegra's company. She's my oldest and best friend. We don't live in each other's pockets. In fact, it's been weeks since we last saw each other. No matter the length of the absence though, we always pick up the thread of our friendship with ease.

Together, we step out of the changing room and head to the pool. I tug at the bikini top, trying to get coverage over my breasts which are spilling over pornographically. Allegra catches my action and laughs, "It's fine, K, leave it alone. Nobody's here to look, although if you want my opinion, it looks tons better on you than on me." That's the thing about Allegra. Always kind, always generous, even if she's stretching the truth, as she must be. Deciding to give up on my modesty, I walk to the edge of the pool and without hesitation, jump in. An echoing splash indicates that Allegra has followed suit. We swim quickly to warm ourselves up, and soon, I feel my body loosen in the welcoming embrace of the water. The stiffness in my shoulders from hours of work at my desk, the tension I've been holding in my ribcage, all of that melts away, and I feel like I'm finally on holiday. Though I won't admit it, Allegra was right to suggest we do this.

We don't linger in the pool, only long enough to swim some lengths, racing from one end to the other, then we laughingly plop into the hot jacuzzi and luxuriate in the warm jets pummelling our bodies. "Ah, that's good," I sigh happily.

"Mmm," agrees Allegra. "One of the perks of visiting home."

I lie back, closing my eyes, and enjoy the bubbling pressure of the water jets on my body. A crackling sound from the speaker on the wall interrupts my pleasure, as Allegra's mum, Lauren, speaks through the intercom, "A, you there?"

"Yes, we've just finished our swim," calls out Allegra.

"Oh, good," says her mum. "I was just calling to let you know dinner will be served in thirty minutes. Don't be late."

"No worries."

"Ok." We both respond at the same time.

The intercom clicks off, and Allegra sits up. "Well," she says, "I suppose we better head upstairs to shower and change."

She steps out of the pool and grabs hold of a towel, draping it over her shoulders then throws another in my direction. I catch it deftly and wrap it sarong-style around my body. I hurry to pick up my bag and clothes from the changing room, then follow Allegra back through the long, glass-covered walkway to the main part of the house. We take a set of steps up to the first floor, traipsing carelessly in our bare feet down a corridor until we reach a set of doors. One of them leads to Allegra's childhood bedroom. Next to it is the guest room where I have stayed on each of my overnight visits.

I'm about to let myself into my room when Allegra stops me hurriedly. "Oh, totally forgot," she cries. "The shower in the guest room is on the blink, so you'll have to share mine." She pauses with a frown. "Time's short though."

The frown eases from her brow as she continues, "I know. Go on and use the bathroom in Wilfred's room. He's not due to arrive until much later, so he won't know, let alone mind."

"You sure?" I ask hesitantly.

"Of course! You know where it is? Just go around the corner and it'll be the first room on your right. Go on."

"Ok," I say, feeling butterflies form in my belly. I have never before ventured into that part of the house. Not that Wilfred lives here anymore, I tell myself. It's just a room that lies empty most of the time. I take the corner then find the first door to my right. Some instinct makes me knock first before I enter. The room is empty, of course. I step inside and take a look around me curiously, but the room is devoid of any personal touches. It's a pleasant-looking space, light and airy, carpeted in cream tones, furnished with a bed, corner desk and a whole wall of floor to ceiling mirror-fronted wardrobes. I'm mildly disappointed though. I had hoped to find some personal footprint of Wilfred's, perhaps some old posters on the wall that tell me of his teenage obsessions. This room, however, is neat and impersonal, almost like in a hotel. Well, what else should I have expected? It's been almost two decades since Wilfred actually lived here.

With an inward shake of my head, I make my way to the en-suite bathroom and quickly start the shower, divesting myself of the ill-fitting bikini. I wash my body briskly, then towel myself dry. Returning to the bedroom, I shuffle in my bag for a fresh set of underwear, placing them on the bed. Then I tug off the towel. I pause as I catch sight of my reflection in the full-length mirror behind me. I turn so I'm facing it fully, and take a moment to inspect myself. The mirror in my own room at home is much smaller, and so I'm rarely afforded the sight of my naked self from top to toe.

I try to be objective. Despite my efforts over the years, I have never managed to achieve a truly slim figure—the kind of figure which would allow me to wear crop tops (if I wanted to) or clothes that fit closely at the waist. I'm not fat, but neither am I slim. There is a roundness to my abdomen, one that translates into belly folds when I'm sitting. My hips flare a little wider than I would wish, and my thighs are thick enough to rub together at the apex. I twirl around and examine my bottom. Not bad, I decide. Could be a lot worse. It's a good handful and nicely rounded with two dimples peeking out at the base of my spine.

I return to gaze at my front. My boobs are definitely the best part of my figure, ample enough to fill a C-cup, with small, dusky-coloured nipples. They haven't given in to the pull of gravity yet and stand perkily enough. Or are they drooping just a little bit? I turn sideways and examine them, cupping them upwards with my palms then letting go to see how much of a drop they take. I do it again, and then once more, so focused on my reflection in the mirror that I don't at first notice the quiet opening of the door. It's not until Wilfred Barton-Browne has fully stepped into the room that I become aware of him and gasp in fright. He comes to a shocked halt, and for a second that stretches far too long in my mind, we both stare at each other, his eyes taking in my naked body on flagrant display.

The next second, he's turning around hastily, giving me his back while I scramble for the towel to restore a modicum of modesty. "Fuck, I'm sorry!" he grunts then adds irritably, "Karima, what the hell are you doing in my room?"

"I—erm—the shower's on the blink," I mumble. "In the guest room," I add, trying for coherence. With one hand, I'm flinging my undies into the bag then picking it up, making sure to keep the towel secure around my middle.

With all my things in hand, I start for the door, saying hurriedly, "Allegra said to use yours. I'm sorry, we weren't expecting you so soon. I'll get out of your hair now." I have to pass him to get to the door, but I keep my gaze down, avoiding his eyes at all costs. Quickly, I let myself out into the hall and scurry like a frightened mouse all the way back to my room.

Chapter 3

I'm falling deeper and deeper

Dressed and ready, I head down to dinner, trying to chase away the tumultuous nerves I'm feeling on the prospect of coming face to face with Wilfred again. God, that was embarrassing! If there's even a hint of knowingness in his eyes when I see him, I know I'm going to be a blushing mess.

As I was getting dressed, I ran over the encounter in my mind. It's not just that he walked in on me naked; he caught me fondling my boobs. What do I say to that? Oh sorry, I was just testing how perky they were. Bloody hell. And to top it all, I had to then give him a full frontal before I had the wherewithal to pull on a towel. What must he have thought? I cringe.

I should shrug it off. It was just a bit of nudity, no biggie. Yeah right. The fact that I'm drowning in embarrassment would indicate the opposite. I wonder if part of the shame I'm feeling has to do with the knowledge that my body is hardly ever going to grace the catwalk. Whereas every single member of the Barton-Browne family is tall and lithe with not an ounce of excess flesh, my frame is on the more petite side at five feet two (and a half), and there is definitely some flesh to spare.

Not that I dislike the way I look. I did for a while in my teens and early twenties, but I've developed more body confidence these past few years. It's important to accept and love oneself, isn't it? Still, all that self-acceptance comes to nothing when someone who is used to far more perfect bodies sets eyes on mine. Agh! I need to shake this off. It happened. It's done. Nothing's changed. I take a deep breath to centre myself and enter the lounge where everyone is congregating before dinner.

Lauren, busy arranging a bauble on the Christmas tree, turns around at my entrance and beams, "Karima, so good to see you." She comes over and brushes her scented cheek to mine in a brief air kiss. "You're looking well, darling. How is the teaching going at your school?"

"Good," I say, now accepting a crushing squeeze of my shoulders from Hugo, his idea of a hug. "As a matter of fact, I got a promotion this term. I've been appointed subject leader for English."

"How wonderful!" exclaims Lauren. She turns to her daughter chidingly, "Why didn't you tell us, A?"

Allegra shrugs her shoulders carelessly. She was one of the first people I told, and we celebrated with a night out last July, but given her infrequent communication with her parents, I'm not surprised the news never reached them. Hugo and Lauren, though kind and generous, are the sort of self-involved couple that are often jetting abroad on holiday, especially now that Hugo has retired from his career as a barrister.

I turn to the final occupant of the room. Wilfred is already on his feet, smiling at me as I approach him hesitantly. "Hey, Karima, it's been a while," he says warmly, wrapping me in a hug. Immediately, I'm engulfed in the headiness of his manly scent. This hug is perfection—firm, comforting and over much too soon. I step back, my heart palpitating wildly in my chest. When am I ever going to get over the crush I have for this gorgeous man? "That's great news about the promotion," he continues as I find a seat to perch on. "How's it been so far?"

There is no change in his manner towards me, a casual brotherly affection, and I breathe an inward sigh of relief. I shouldn't have got into a tizzy about that encounter upstairs. He's obviously moved past it. I give a small smile. "It's increased my workload no end, but in a good way. I've always wanted to have a go at something like this." Raising literacy standards is a cause close to my heart and one of the reasons I went into teaching in the first place.

"I can't think of anyone better suited for the job," Wilfred states forthrightly.

"Hear, hear," concurs Hugo.

I feel a warm tingle at the praise. When I had put my hat into the ring for this promotion, I hadn't thought I would get it. There were other teachers more senior than me who had their eye on the position. It was therefore a very happy surprise to have been selected, and something I don't take for granted at all. It's been the most positive thing that happened to me all year, the pay rise finally allowing me to take the plunge and buy my own home.

I've spent the last few months alternating between teaching, slaving at my desk over the new English curriculum I want to introduce, and working to update my house which was a fixer upper I got for a steal at auction. It helps that my brother is a kitchen fitter by trade. Whenever he's had a spare moment, he's been over at my place, installing a fancy-looking kitchen, shelves in the sitting room and wardrobes upstairs. My nesting instinct has been in full force. If at times, I've felt an ache to have some significant other sharing that nest with me, I've forcibly pushed the feeling away. I'm incredibly lucky and much more fortunate than most. I've got a good job and a good home; but still missing the life partner. Two out of three ain't bad, according to Meatloaf. I shouldn't complain.

The conversation easily moves on to other topics and soon, we're seating ourselves at the dining table. I find myself next to Wilfred, his presence once more setting my pulse beating double time. All through the meal, I'm intensely conscious of his presence beside me. From the corner of my eyes, I study his hands as he uses his cutlery. They're large but well-shaped, with long fingers and neatly trimmed nails. I find my attention occupied by the smattering of dark hair peeking out from the cuff at his wrist. Two veins run down the broad back of his hands, hinting at strength and power. My mind wanders to what those thick and strong digits could do to my body in the throes of passion. I feel heat stain my cheeks. Oh crap. I need to get ahold of myself.

Wilfred is reaching out for the wine bottle. "Would you like a top up?" he enquires.

I shake my head. I don't have a great tolerance for alcohol, and the two glasses I've had are more than enough. "No thanks," I say. "I think I've reached my limit." He smiles understandingly and goes on to replenish the drinks for the other people at the table.

When he's done, he settles beside me again and asks quietly, "So, what has been your first priority as subject leader for English?"

I take a sip of water before I reply, "There's two areas I'm keen to improve: pedagogy and curriculum." His interested gaze encourages me to go on. "Our outcomes are good at Key Stage 1, but attainment drops off sharply as the students get older, especially in extended writing tasks. I think we need to address that gap."

"What do you propose to do about it?"

"You really want to know?"

He quirks his lips. "I really want to know."

I take him at his word and proceed to tell him about my plans. He intersperses my narrative with the occasional question that tells me he's really listening, and I won't lie, it feels good to be truly seen and heard. Hugo, Lauren and Allegra listen in and comment too, but it's Wilfred's keen regard that drives me to expound and speak at greater length than I otherwise would. His face is creased in concentration as he listens intently. I realise that I've been hogging attention for far too long and bring my speech to a hasty end. He nods thoughtfully. "If you want my penny's worth, Karima, I think you're on to something there. Go with it and good luck."

"Thanks," I say, feeling tongue-tied now that I've rabbited on for so long.

"Definitely on the right track," Allegra nods decisively. "Stick with it and don't let any naysayers derail you."

I snort, "Easier said than done. Institutional resistance to change is well-known."

Wilfred angles towards me, his leg bumping gently against mine under the table. I'm burning inside. Burning. "Rome wasn't built in a day," he says, his quiet growl making the nether regions of my body quiver and ache. "The trick is to keep going with dogged perseverance, Karima, adapting when you need to, but never losing sight of the main goal you want to achieve. Having listened to you just now, I can tell you have the knowledge, the passion, but most importantly, the mental clarity to see this through." He smiles and adds encouragingly, "I'm sure you'll get there." Oh dear Lord, this man. In my life, I've been too used to people—outside my family and Allegra— shooting down my big ideas, and now, here is someone doing the opposite, bigging me up and cheering me on. I feel myself falling deeper and deeper into this chronic crush I have for Wilfred. It's going to take much more than a few days this time to get back into even a semblance of an even keel.

Lauren comes to the rescue just then, thank goodness. "How about pudding?" she asks.

We all hasten to say yes, and the topic of my career is dropped. All through the rest of the evening though, I feel Wilfred's gaze on me. Has he always looked at me this way, or is this something new? Am I dreaming this up, my fantasies overriding reality? I must be. He couldn't be. Interested in me that is. I mean, the guy is so far out of my reach that the idea of him fancying me is nothing short of fanciful. Don't get me wrong. I know my worth—I practise self-love after all—but I also live in the real world. I know how things are with rich, handsome, successful men. They have gorgeous women flock to them without even lifting a finger. In the grand scheme of things, I'm merely a tiny pawn enjoying a moment of his attention. It would be very foolish indeed to make anything more out of it.

That doesn't stop me from retiring to bed that night in a haze of contentment and to fall asleep to dreams of Wilfred, and what his strong hands could do to my needy body.

Chapter 4

Get a grip, Karima

Christmas morning, I wake and luxuriate dreamily in my ongoing fantasy starring Wilfred Barton-Browne. This one's an X-rated version of it that has my hand sneaking down inside my pyjamas and stroking my clit until I'm so needy for release that I turn over, bunching the covers between my legs for extra friction, and dry hump the bed, smothering my cry of ecstasy into the pillow when I come.

I pant breathlessly, heat spreading through my body as I guiltily come back to my senses. Time for a reality check if there ever was one. Blowing out a frustrated breath, I push myself off the bed and go to clean away the evidence of my depraved imaginings, before dressing and heading downstairs. On the way to the large eat-in kitchen, I give myself a pep talk. Keep these feelings in check, Karima. Once Christmas is over, we'll part ways and I probably won't see Wilfred again for ages. This is just a case of a childhood crush verging on hero worship, lethally mixed in with the intense pheromones of animal attraction. It will all dissipate once I'm gone from here, and life will go back to normal. Best focus on that.

No sooner do I catch sight of Wilfred sitting at the counter nursing a hot cup of coffee than all my good intentions go flying by the wayside. My eyes, seemingly with a will of their own, fix on the broad expanse of his chest under the ridiculously cheesy Christmas jumper he's wearing. Even with that get-up, he looks yummy, and oh so unattainable. I cast my eyes down, mumbling a good morning to everyone, and busy myself with pouring some coffee.

When I go to sit down, there's only one available bar stool at the kitchen counter—the one beside Wilfred. I carefully set my coffee cup down, not meeting his eyes, and do my level best to climb on to the swivelling stool as gracefully as I can. Bar stools are a pet hate of mine. You won't find any in my kitchen, that's for sure. These things are made for tall people, who can casually perch their bums on them with no effort at all. For people like me, it's an ungainly leap up to get myself situated, followed by a sustained effort at maintaining my balance since my feet are unable to reach the floor. If ever there were a discriminatory piece of furniture, then it would be the bar stool, and I'd be perfectly willing to write a thesis on the matter.

The ungraceful clamber onto my seat is made all the worse as I can feel Wilfred's eyes on me. Then he has the temerity to ask, "Sleep well?" which only serves to remind me of my lustful dreams and to paint my face with an unbecoming flush.

"Very well, thanks," I mutter, then clam up and say not a single more word throughout breakfast.

Christmas mornings in the Barton-Browne household are relaxed and laid-back. We have a light breakfast, then open presents, after which we usually take a long walk along the river, ending up for a drink at the Black Lion pub. Only then do we head back to the house for our Christmas dinner.

With breakfast over, we decamp to the living room and start handing out wrapped parcels to each other. This year, we've been under strict instructions from Lauren that all gifts have to be under £5 and should at least be partly made by our own hands. I suppose it's her way to inject a more personal touch to the annual gift giving process, but it's been a damned nuisance. When do I have the time or space or even the will to craft some gifts? To be fair, Christmas gift shopping for the Barton-Brownes has always been a challenge. What do you get for people who already have everything they could possibly need? Toiletries? They'd be gracefully accepted only to then be unobtrusively donated to the local charity shop.

In the end, I settled for home-made truffles which I packaged neatly into little boxes with the uninspired message, "A festive treat from me to you, Karima". In this endeavour, I made use of the knowledge I gained at a chocolate-making workshop I attended last spring, the voucher for which had been Hugo and Lauren Barton-Browne's present to me the previous Christmas. There is a pleasing symmetry in the idea of returning the favour by offering them the fruits of my newly acquired expertise.

I watch Wilfred carefully, without being overt about it, as he opens the box and glimpses the chocolates inside. Without prompting, he pops one into his mouth, and his eyes close briefly as he makes pleasurable noises.

"These are excellent," he says, already reaching for another.

Around me, the rest of the Barton-Brownes concur with this assessment, but it's Wilfred I focus on. He gobbles up the second truffle, then looks straight at me. "Thank you," he says simply, and the warmth of his gaze sets off a million butterflies in my belly. *Get a grip, Karima, get a grip.*

I look down at the package in my hands and begin to unwrap it. Wilfred's gift to me is a personalised mug filled to the brim with Mejdool dates stuffed with almonds. How did he know they're my favourites? On the mug, he's drawn some goofy artwork—clearly, Allegra's not the only person in the family with an artistic bent—and added the corny message, "It's time for a cuppa, says your bestie's brotha". Okay, so I'm not the only one coming up short on the clever puns front. That's a relief, given my less than stellar efforts on the do-it-yourself gift. Admiring the mug in my hands, I know, of course, that it's going to take pride of place in my kitchen.

I look across at Wilfred. "This is so pretty," I tell him with a smile, "and these dates are my favourites too. Thank you!"

"You're welcome," he says, then holds up the box of truffles I made, "though it's not a patch on these." His gaze is a tad sheepish, and for once, he seems a little less than his usual suave and composed self—less of an unattainable hero and more human, more endearing. The flutters in my belly turn to something more searing. For a brief moment, I'm gripped by the sense that something is dislodging in my neatly ordered life. Then the moment passes, as Allegra makes some humorous remark that has everyone chuckling.

With the present giving done, we're soon heading out for a walk along the river path. The day is crisp and cool but dry, perfect for a leisurely stroll. Hugo and Lauren walk ahead of us, while in the rearguard there's me, Allegra and Wilfred.

I listen absently to their conversation. Although there's an eight-year gap between them, Allegra and Wilfred are close. I think they're bound, among other things, by the single-mindedness of their artistic temperament; Wilfred with the passionate way he pursues his movie projects, and

Allegra with the intensity of her focus on her art. When these two are taken up by a project, they go all in. For weeks, Allegra will be incommunicado if she's working on paintings for a forthcoming exhibition. And from the sounds of it, Wilfred is similarly inclined. I've watched him this past day regularly checking his phone and typing out messages, or going outside briefly for a phone call. All of it speaks of the high-powered movie mogul.

As he tells his sister about this new movie, *Ruin*, which he's producing, I feel the intensity of his desire to see this project come to life despite what seem to be insurmountable obstacles in the way. They don't appear to put him off at all, only to rekindle his resolve. I wish I could be a smidgeon more like that. Maybe then I wouldn't be constantly second guessing myself. Self-doubt follows me at every turn. Am I good enough for this role? Is my strategy right? What if I push through my plan and find it was the wrong thing to do? Rationally, I can tell myself until I'm blue in the face that I've read the research, that there is plenty of evidence that my proposed approach will work, that it could help transform lives for the better. There will always be an element of doubt in my mind. In contrast, both Allegra and Wilfred show a self-belief that I envy.

I suppose that's why they're so successful in their respective fields and highly respected, both of them earning eye-watering sums of money. I am so out of their league. I think back to the way I spoke about my curriculum plans last night and feel a teensy bit embarrassed. My work is small fry compared to theirs, or it appears to be at least. I am not going to do down the heroic endeavours of teachers up and down this country. What we do is important. Still, I can't help feeling a bit small in comparison. And as for any romantic ambitions I might have harboured last night for sexy as sin Wilfred, or just now as we were exchanging gifts—well in the full light of day, I can see them for the pipe dream they really are.

As we round the bend to take us to the Black Lion pub, I urge myself to snap out of this self-pitying train of thought. So what if I'm out of their league? Why should I compete with them? Wouldn't it be better to stick to my own lane and excel there? Simultaneously, I tell myself that it's time to do something proactive about my single state. If I had someone to warm my bed at night, I wouldn't be wasting my time on crazy fantasies about Wilfred. Well, I decide, a decent man is not going to materialise on my front door out of nowhere. If I want to end my singledom, I have to do something about it, even if it means I have to enter the lion pit of online dating. It's all the rage now, isn't it? Might as well give it a try.

"You're very quiet," remarks Allegra. I feel Wilfred's eyes on me.

"Nah," I say with a nonchalant smile, "just being a good listener. Didn't want to hog the limelight."

"Hmm," she murmurs, unconvinced.

We enter the pub, and Wilfred turns to me. "What will you have?"

"A diet Coke, please." He nods, enquires of the others then goes off to order our drinks at the bar.

As we settle ourselves down, Allegra focuses on me once more. "So, what's been going on in your head? I can tell there's something fermenting."

"Been thinking of some new year resolutions," I reply.

"Go on."

I tick them off on my fingers. "One, stop letting self-doubt undermine my efforts at work."

"Yep, good one," agrees Allegra. "What else you got?"

"Two, end my single state asap."

"What's the plan?" queries my friend.

I let out a gentle sigh. "Give online dating a try, I suppose."

"Ooh, I saw something about it on the news the other day," pipes in Lauren, looking much too interested for my liking. "It's the next big thing, apparently. In a few years' time, everyone's going to be dating online as if it's totally normal. Do give it a try!" She adds in a whisper, "Then tell us all about it." Hugo nods his head in agreement.

"It can't hurt," opines Allegra. She cocks her head to one side, inspecting me. "Now's as good a time as any to get started. You're looking very fetching in that reindeer jumper. How about I snap a photo of you for your profile? Your new phone has a camera, doesn't it?"

I put a self-conscious hand up to my messy hair, but Allegra flicks it away. "Stop that. You look fab."

"Indeed you do," agrees Lauren with a smile. She holds out her hand. "Give me your phone and I'll take a photo, if you'll show me how."

I can hardly say no, can I? Reluctantly, I hand over my phone and give quick instructions about which button to press. I sit up straight as Lauren focuses the phone camera on me. "Smile," she instructs.

I try a slight smile, not showing my teeth. "Wider," Lauren snaps authoritatively. I force a wider grin, all the while squirming inside. "There," she says with satisfaction and gives me back my phone. I check the photos, Allegra looking over my shoulder.

"That one," she decides. I can't fault her judgement. The photo is somewhat flattering.

It's at this moment that Wilfred comes back, bearing our drinks. "What are you all looking at?" he asks curiously while setting out the drinks on the table.

Hugo answers for me. "We've just taken some photos of Karima for her online dating profile."

Wilfred's gaze flies to me, and do I detect a tightening of his lips? If so, he can stick his judginess up his backside. Us lesser mortals must make do with the means at our disposal. We can't all have our pick of gorgeous people flocking to us.

"May I see?" he asks, his voice flat.

I show him the photo on my phone. As he leans close to inspect it, I inhale the scent of him, wondering idly what cologne he uses that smells so good. He gazes at the photo for a second or two. "Nice," he says shortly. "What website are you using?"

I shrug, not really wanting to discuss the topic any further. "Dunno. I'll have to do a spot of research when I have a spare moment."

"You'll be careful, won't you?" Wilfred asks, narrowing his gaze on me. "Only meet people in public places and always let Allegra know where you're going."

"Of course," I reply, wishing the ground would swallow me up. This is simply too embarrassing.

"Just don't get cold feet and abandon the whole thing," chides Allegra.

"I won't," I say, picking up my drink. "Now, how about a toast?"

Allegra clinks her glass to mine. "To Karima finding love next year," she says with a smile.

"I'll drink to that," agrees Hugo.

"To Karima finding love," echoes Lauren.

Wilfred doesn't say anything, but gently taps his glass to mine. "I had in mind something more general," I explain, a little flustered, "like drinking to everyone's good health and happiness."

"We can drink to that too," responds Hugo jovially, and we clink our glasses again. Thankfully then the conversation moves on to other topics.

Chapter 5

Chilling in front of the telly sounds heavenly

The week after Christmas I spend mostly at home. I decorate the spare bedroom upstairs. I sand and polish the floors. I read paperback romances I picked up from the charity shop. What I don't do is set up a profile on a dating website. For some reason, I keep putting that off. I tell myself it's because I'm still in the throes of my hopeless crush on Wilfred Barton-Browne, and that once a few weeks have passed, I'll be in a better frame of mind to tackle the subject of dating again.

I haven't made any plans for New Year's Eve, except to chill at home with some comfort food and watch a movie. Allegra's in Edinburgh with her current flame, going to some party or other then watching the fireworks on Princes Street. She called two days ago and tried to convince me to join her in the Scottish capital, but I said no. I've already had enough of being the charity case; I really don't need to add to that by playing third wheel. Besides, I'd much rather cosy up under a blanket on my nice new couch than be outside in this cold and miserable weather. Grr... just thinking about it makes me shiver.

My brother called too, checking in on me from Poland. He made disgruntled noises about my turning into a hermit cat lady, which is ridiculous. I'm planning to start dating, aren't I? Only not just yet. This holiday season is not the time to signal to the world my aloneness. Though the idea of getting a cat is not a bad one. I could do with some feline company at home.

It's half past nine, and I'm in my kitchen clearing away the detritus from the Chinese take-out I had for dinner. One of the advantages of eating solo like this is that I didn't have to share any of the pancakes for the crispy duck, which in my experience are always in short supply. A win for me. There's a marble cake on the kitchen counter, which I plan to have later with a cup of tea. I could have baked something more fancy to mark the festive new year, but this morish cake is just the type of comfort food I need while I watch a movie on the couch. My evening is all set.

Then the phone rings.

As I hurry to grab it from a side table in the living room, I wonder who could be calling me at this time on New Year's Eve. The initials I see on the screen—WBB—have me pause in confusion. My next reaction is one of worry. It must be bad news, something to do with the family. Why else would Wilfred be calling? My hand trembles as I put the phone to my ear. Could it be Allegra? In a low and shaky voice, I breathe, "Hello?"

"Hey, Karima, it's Wilfred."

"Hi," I manage, my heart and mind racing.

"How are you doing?"

Why is he taking forever to get to the point? If it's bad news, I wish he would just spit it out. In the background, I can hear muted voices and music. He doesn't sound like he's at a hospital. My confusion increases, so all I can do is mumble, "Good thanks. You?"

"Yeah, all good here," he replies, dousing my worries though leaving me still very confused. "Listen," he goes on to say, "I wanted to be one of the first to wish you a happy new year."

"Oh." I am flummoxed for a moment, then I gather myself. "Thanks. Happy new year to you too." There is an awkward pause. What else is there to discuss? All I can think to say is, "Sounds like you're at a party."

"Yeah," he says, stretching out the vowel. "And you? Have a fun evening lined up?"

I smile to myself. "You could say that."

It's almost as if he hears that smile, for his tone grows hesitant. "I—well, I won't keep you from your plans, Karima. Just wanted to touch base and wish you well." Then, out of the blue, he adds, "Maybe we can catch up in the new year some time."

What is this bizarre new incarnation of Wilfred Barton-Browne? I have never heard him talk like this. Mystified, I mumble, "Sure. Take care now and thanks for calling."

"You too, take care, and Happy New Year."

For several minutes after he ends the call, I stare at the phone in my hand, not quite understanding what it is that has just taken place. This didn't feel like a casual call at all. Wilfred sounded... not like his usual self. I can't quite shake off the thought that he wanted something from me. I'm almost tempted to dial his number and ask what's up, but even I'm not that courageous. With a sigh, I put the phone down and settle on my couch, reaching for the remote. I spend a minute or two idly scrolling through the movie listings, trying to pick something to watch, but my mind is not wholly focused on the task. I keep playing back that strange phone conversation.

Something's wrong. I can feel it. Wilfred sounded... forlorn, for lack of a better word. I can't pretend to know what's going on with him, but I can sense instinctively that something is causing him distress, and for some reason, he felt the need to reach out to me. I can't let it go. To hell with my cowardliness; I need to call him back.

My hand is reaching for the phone when it begins to ring again, and I see it's Wilfred. I don't hesitate. I pick up straight away. "Wilfred," I say.

He speaks at the same time. "Karima."

I rush on, "You ok?"

I hear him let out a deep breath. "Yes, I'm fine. It's just—sorry if this seems odd and presumptuous, but could I join you tonight, wherever you are?"

"I—of course you can," I say, a little taken aback. "Though I'm afraid I'm not out anywhere interesting tonight. I'm at home chilling in front of the TV."

"That sounds heavenly," he replies fervently.

"Not feeling the party vibe tonight?" I enquire sympathetically.

"No, in fact, I've just broken out and made my escape. Chilling in front of the telly sounds much more the thing."

I laugh. "Well in that case, do come over. I can offer you a comfy couch, home-baked cake, a warm drink and your choice of movie on Sky."

"Perfect. I'll grab a bottle of bubbly on the way. See you in about twenty minutes. Oh, and Karima—"

"Yes?" I ask when he pauses.

"Don't do a single thing in the meantime. I mean, if your place is a tip—not that I'm implying it is—then leave it just as it is. Carry on with your evening just as you had planned; don't pander in any way to the person who's had the cheek to invite himself over at the last minute."

I cast a look around me. The house looks alright, though I'd be tempted to give the duster a brisk run over the surfaces and to plump up some cushions. Maybe also a quick vacuum?

I sigh. "You do realise you're asking me to disregard the houseproud part of my nature."

He gives an amused snort. "Perhaps, but please don't put yourself out just because I'm coming over. I'm imposing enough as it is."

"No, you're not."

It's quiet for a time on the other end of the line, then he says softly, "See you in a bit."

As soon as the call ends, I'm on my feet, agitation and excitement warring within me. Wilfred is coming to my house. Oh my God. Wilfred! I dash to the bathroom and give everything a quick sanitising wipe, then place a fresh hand towel on the rack. Back in my room, I run a coat of deodorant under my armpits and consider changing clothes. I'm in my usual lounge wear of soft yoga pants and baggy sweater. In the end, I decide against it. The last thing I want is to look as if I'm trying too hard, though I do give my hair a brush and put on some lip balm.

Reflexively, I straighten the covers on my bed, however unlikely it is that he'll even set foot in this room. This is not a date. He is not coming over for seduction. He just needs a bit of friendly company that's all. I bet it can't be easy or relaxing being around movie types all the time. At least it wouldn't be for me. I don't suppose it's any different for Wilfred, despite all his undoubted career success. I've watched him closely over the years. Whenever he visits home, he's a bit brittle at first, carrying over some nervous tension. Then, as the visit progresses, I see him relax and become more at ease, playful even.

Producing multi-million dollar movies can be a stressful business. No wonder he feels the need at times to get away from it all and be himself with his family. Since Allegra's in Scotland and his parents are holidaying in Gstaad, I realise in surprise that I'm the remaining family he has here in London. It's a heartwarming feeling to know he's turned to me, and I'm determined to offer him a relaxing and stress-free evening at my place. I won't read anything more into his visit tonight. I won't get romantic notions. It's enough that he's reached out, that he wants to be here. The thought that I can in some small way be of solace to him floods me with happiness. Wilfred is coming over to spend New Year's Eve with me. Now isn't that a turn up for the books?

PART TWO: WILFRED

Chapter 6

✦ ♥ ✦

An epiphany in Los Angeles

Present day

He sat in the plush airport lounge, a cool can of beer at his fingertips, and considered sending her a text message. He hesitated. She sometimes kept the phone next to the radio on the bedside table, especially if she was alone at night. Other times she charged it on the kitchen counter. It was late in London right now, in the early hours of the morning. The buzz of an incoming message might wake her if she had the phone nearby, and that was the last thing she needed when she had work the next morning.

Reluctantly, he put the phone down and took a long pull of his beer. They should be calling his flight any minute now. It was scheduled to land at Heathrow at 12:30 the following day, which should give him plenty of time to set his plan in motion. To be on the safe side, he picked up the phone again and this time, sent a message to Hamid, whom he suspected would still be awake, even at such a late hour.

Wilfred: Coming back from LA early to surprise mum. Can you make yourself scarce tomorrow evening? Maybe go over to Uncle Amir or Allegra's. I'll make it up to you.

Hamid: Cool. I'm in need of a new telephoto lens for my camera. There's one for sale at £150

Wilfred: Mercenary!

Hamid: Just doing you a solid

Wilfred: Send me the link for the lens and I'll have a think about how we can make this work. I'm not handing over the cash just like that.

Hamid: Sending now

Wilfred: Thanks. Now go to sleep. It's late and you've got school tomorrow.

There was no response to that, which could be taken to mean one of two things. Either Hamid had indeed settled down to sleep (unlikely) or he thought it beneath him to respond to that last message. Wilfred chuckled to himself as he put the phone down and took a last swig of his beer.

He hadn't planned to be travelling tonight. In fact, there were several important meetings scheduled for tomorrow. It made no logical sense for him to be returning home ahead of schedule—except, it totally did. The decision had been made earlier today. He'd been in a fraught, three-way meeting between himself, the director on the set of his latest movie, and the studio executives who wanted at this very late stage to make big changes to the script based on some pre-emptive market research they had undertaken— regardless of the fact that his production company's contract with the studio, brought in to help finance this big budget movie, was watertight and did not give them the right to interfere with the artistic integrity of the project after shooting had begun. Still, it didn't stop them from trying.

He'd had the director spewing angry words into one ear, at one point threatening to walk out on the project, and the studio executives laying down their demands in the other ear and threatening to withhold important funds that were due later this month. Back and forth it went, with Wilfred trying to appease both sides while keeping a sharp eye on making sure the project itself didn't self-destruct. The voices in his ear had grown to a cacophony, and closing his eyes briefly, he'd had a vision of Karima, lying lonely in their marital bed back home. He'd felt a stab of intense pain at the thought. "Why the fuck am I here?" he'd wondered to himself. He'd felt strangely detached from the proceedings around him, almost as if he were outside his own body. It was not the first time he'd experienced such a thing. It had happened years ago, precipitating the most important decision of his life. And then, just as he had done two decades ago, he'd stood, preparing to leave.

"Walter," he'd said, addressing the fuming director. "You walk out on this project, and you won't work in this business again. You know it, so stop the empty threats. We'll keep to the script and stay on track until we see the footage at the halfway mark, as planned."

He'd turned then to the studio executives. "If you have any issue with this, you better get your lawyers on standby for the lawsuit that'll come your way should you renege on the terms agreed."

Packing up his laptop and papers into his bag, he'd smiled at Irene, his co-producer and junior partner in the production company he'd founded. "Irene, I'm heading back to London to be with my wife. You're more than capable of handling the rest from here. Keep me informed and speak soon." And he'd walked out of the meeting room to the dumbfounded stares of all the people around him.

It had felt good to kick back at the noise and just simply do the right thing, which was to go home and be with his family, movie project be damned. He had enough wherewithal to know that in time, all these problems would get ironed out, and the movie would get made. Too much was at stake to throw the baby out with the bath water. Time with his loved ones, on the other hand, was not something he could ever get back. And so he had felt no doubt instructing the limo driver to take him straight to the airport, making a phone call along the way to change his flight booking.

He'd spent the last hour in the airport lounge on the phone, dealing with the fallout from his unexpected departure. But it was time now to board the plane. He stood and stretched, feeling weary yet content. With purposeful steps, he boarded the plane and settled into his business class seat. Once airborne, he got comfortable, nestled into his pillow and closed his eyes to sleep, his mind drifting to that time, years ago, when everything changed.

20 years previously

Chapter 7

What's my why?

Christmas Eve

I'm tense and on edge. The past few weeks have been full on, and I'm reaching the limits of my endurance. My work is never stress-free at the best of times, but this latest movie I'm producing has been riddled with challenges. When the novel, *Ruin*, first came out last year, I just knew I wanted to make it into a movie. People thought I was mad. The story could not translate to the big screen. It was too quirky, had too many disparate timelines, morally grey heroes, an ambiguous ending—basically all the things that the Hollywood industry avoids like the plague.

But I have a vision in my mind of how I could make it work, one that has not wavered since I took this project on. First, there were long negotiations with the sceptical author to buy the movie rights. We got through that hump. And now, we're on to the actual script, which is going through re-write after re-write, not to mention three different script writers. We're making some headway with it, but it's been tough. No one said turning this novel into a movie would be a walk in the park.

I'm sitting with my team around the table, script in hand while we go at it scene by scene. We still have a mountain of work to do, but for the past hour, we've been going round and round in circles, lacking inspiration, not making any visible progress. We're supposed to keep going until seven tonight, though I've seen several people glance longingly at their phones and type out quick messages to family and friends. Everyone clearly wishes to go home and start their holiday. I sigh out loud and give in. "Ok folks, let's leave it there and meet up again after Christmas. I can see you're all dying to go."

There is a collective murmur of relief around me, and everyone quickly disperses, wishing each other a merry Christmas. Now that we've stopped for the day, I'm eager too to get going. Within minutes, I'm in my car, speeding down the A4 towards Chiswick, where mum and dad live. As I drive along in the afternoon traffic, I feel the tension slowly seep from my body. Music plays from the car's CD player, an album by a new band called Keane which I've been listening to lately. I sing along to the chorus of *Everybody's Changing*, where the singer bemoans the fact that everyone except for him seem to be moving on with their lives. I can relate. In the past year, two of my best friends from university have finally tied the knot. Another friend became a dad for the first time. I'm thirty-six, so that's hardly surprising. It's that time in life where everyone seems to have settled down—except for me.

There's no need for any self-pity. I'm living the life: a successful high-powered career in the movie industry, a swanky house in Notting Hill, a string of pretty girlfriends. Aren't I the lucky one? Okay, so I do know that not having a significant other makes all the material stuff seem shallow by contrast. I'm not emotionally stunted. I also know that for more years than I can remember, I've been singularly focused on getting ahead, on becoming a success. And I've achieved it all, though I'm not resting on my laurels. There are still more successes to aspire to;

getting *Ruin* made and staying true to my vision of it; earning more accolades; maximising box office returns. But fundamentally, I'm there where I want to be, so what now? More of the same? I wouldn't be human if I didn't crave something more.

Perhaps that thing about everybody changing except for me isn't strictly true. I have made changes, the biggest one being the move back to the UK after many years stateside. The decision came shortly after mum had a minor health scare that made me sit up and take stock. I'd also recently broken up with a semi long-term girlfriend. Late one night, reading some self-help book she'd left behind in my condo, I'd come across a passage which basically said that all people have one origin story, one "why" for their entire life, and that why goes back to how they were raised. What was my "why"?

Here's the funny thing about me. Everyone thinks I'm some privileged asshole who grew up in an aristocratic family with a silver spoon in my mouth, attending the most exclusive schools and then going on to study at Oxford. And they would be right, but also wrong.

It's not common knowledge, as mum likes to downplay this period in our lives, but I was born Wilfred O'Dowd and brought up on a council estate in Woolwich. By the time I reached my first birthday, my feckless father was well out of the picture, though he left me his blue eyes and dark hair as a legacy. For many years, it was just me and mum. Then she met Hugo Barton-Browne, and they fell in love. Almost overnight, I exchanged a poky flat in Woolwich for a great mansion on Chiswick Mall as my home. A wedding and a year later, I took on the name Barton-Browne and became a doting brother to my new baby sister, Allegra.

I learned soon enough to erase all trace of a south London accent from my voice. A tutor was brought in to help coach me for the 11+ entrance exam to an exclusive public school. I aced it and forged a path onwards through school to Oxford University and all the Hollywood success I've had since, never looking back, only forward.

Though I've never forgotten those early days on the estate. They're still there, in the back recesses of my mind—the many hours I spent next door at Mr and Mrs Ghani's flat playing with their son, Hamid, who was the same age as me, the aromatic spices that hung in the air while Mrs Ghani cooked in their tiny kitchen, the meals I ate there, exquisitely spiced kebabs wrapped in delicious flatbread, flavoursome Kabuli rice and tender lamb. It was a far cry from the beans on toast and Spag Bol that mum made from a jar of supermarket sauce. Those were happy times I spent with the Ghanis next door. I was always a bit disappointed when mum would come to fetch me at the end of each day. I wanted to stay in the happy bubble that was their home.

Then came the disruption of our move to a mansion in Chiswick, and I never saw the Ghanis again after that. I was deposited in a world alien to me, and thereafter, all my energy became focused on fitting in, on metamorphosing into Wilfred Barton-Browne, a man of wealth, power and influence. And here I am today. I suppose that answers the question as to what is my "why", but not entirely. Those happy days with the Ghanis, eating at the table together, listening to stories Mr Ghani told about his work as a taxi driver, making up new and creative games to play with Hamid—all those memories have never left me. That night in LA, thumbing through the self-help book, it came to me that my greatest "why" was wanting to re-create that happy home I experienced at the Ghanis. In a moment of surprising insight, I realised that each and every one of the movies or tv shows I'd produced had, somewhere along the dramatic storylines, a version of that happy home. And if I wanted something of that for myself, I would have to return to my roots somehow.

So, I took the first step and moved back to London. But old habits die hard. I soon began dating again, an endless line of beautiful women, none of whom stood a chance of recreating that kind of happy home with me. I suppose I still have lots of work to do on myself. Perhaps I should embrace the California thing and start seeing a therapist. I snort. Fat chance.

Checking my far-side mirror, I indicate to change lanes and exit the A4. With a quiet sigh, I put aside the introspection. There'll be time enough for that. For now, there's Christmas with mum, dad, Allegra and Karima to look forward to. Ah yes, Karima, my guilty little pleasure.

I've always had a bit of a soft spot for her. She's by far and away the only friend of Allegra's I've ever had any time for. I've admired the way she conducts herself with quiet dignity despite the obvious fact she doesn't feel at ease in our posh surroundings. She doesn't speak much, but when she does, in a gentle lilt that hints at her Afghan heritage, she does so with well-considered intelligence. It doesn't take a genius to figure out she must feel like an outsider among us, with our double-barrelled name and upper-crusty lifestyle. I suppose it takes one to know one, as I'm just as much of a misfit, though I learned early on to mask it.

Perhaps that's why I've felt some sort of affinity for Karima from the moment we met. She reminds me indirectly of my old friends, the dark inkiness of her beautiful eyes and soft lilt in her voice speaking of sweet familiarity, giving me a sense of that happy home I used to seek out as a child. But she's my sister's best friend and pretty much out of bounds, not to mention, our lifestyles are a world apart. She's not the kind of girl I make the moves on, but that doesn't detract from the sweet though brief pleasure I'll get from enjoying her company this Christmas. I park my car next to her old Ford Fiesta, a smile forming on my lips. It's good to be home.

Chapter 8

◄——— ♥ ———►

Hell, what am I doing?

I let myself into the house with my spare key and dash upstairs to deposit my overnight bag in my room. I'm barely through the door when I come to an abrupt halt. My eyes zero in on the sight of a naked woman standing sideways to the mirror and palming her generous breasts, then letting them go with a delectable bounce. She turns to face me with a shocked gasp, and in a flash, I get an eyeful of the rest of her—soft curves and caramel skin, brown-tipped nipples delightfully puckered up, and further down, an intriguing patch of neatly trimmed black hair. At the same time, I realise this bountifully fleshed woman is Karima.

Next moment, I'm turning around quickly to spare her blushes as she stammers an apology for being in my room, something about the shower being on the blink in hers. I hear the rustle as she drapes a towel around herself and collects all her things. Two seconds later, she rushes out of the room, head cast down in shame and embarrassment.

For a minute, I stand as if turned to stone. Stone being the operative word as I'm rock hard. It's the throbbing of my cock, which strains against the zipper of my jeans, that finally wakes me from my stupor. Fuck. I hastily rearrange myself and lay a calming hand over my raging erection, trying to get the image of a naked Karima out of my mind. She's my little sister's friend, damn it, and I should not be having pervy thoughts about her. But goddamn. That was one of the hottest things I've seen in a while.

Karima. Get your head out of the gutter, Wilfred. That is your sister's best friend, a shy, introverted girl who's had it tough, losing both her mum and dad before she turned twenty. She's not a girl though, not anymore, but a fully grown woman. And fuck, she's sexy. I'm so turned on my dick is taking ages to stand down. All because I got a quick flash of her in the buff.

I rake restless fingers through my hair. Let's be honest here. I'm no stranger to naked women. No stranger even to beautiful naked women, in the industry that I work in. But mostly, the nudity I see is of the slim-bordering-on-skinny and immaculately groomed variety. When was the last time I even saw a woman with pubic hair? Far longer than I can recall. It's all bare, bare, bare down there these days. But the sight of Karima in all her naked glory has shaken me. All at once, I felt a visceral urge both to devour her and to sink into the softness of her fragrant flesh. As she passed me on her way out of the room, leaving a trail of her scent wafting invitingly towards me, I was tempted for a crazy instant to do just that. Yeah, that would have been interesting to say the least. Fortunately, good sense prevailed.

Who'd have thought it? *Karima.* Yes, I've always had a soft spot for her, but my feelings have been of the brotherly, affectionate sort. Right? They could hardly have been anything else. When we first met, she was a young girl of twelve or thirteen, while I was already into the second year of my degree at Oxford and had a girlfriend. I came home only briefly for the holidays and the occasional weekend, so I didn't see all that much of her. She's grown into adulthood since then, but she's always been so quiet and demure in my presence that I've never had occasion to think of her in any way other than platonically as my sister's best friend. Okay, that's not quite true. I have had the occasional non-platonic thoughts about her, but those I resolutely hammered back into their hole each time they popped up, like a mental game of whack-a-mole.

It's safe to say that my platonic-only notion of her has been blown out of the water. I can never unsee those lush breasts cupped in her hands, and their enticing jiggle as she set them free. But seriously, there's nowhere to go with this except to cast the memory into the dustheap. I'm sure Karima must be feeling mortified enough about all this without my making things any worse for her. I will be a gentleman and never allude to it again. I just need my recalcitrant cock to receive the memo.

I lean on my two elbows and hang my head down, breathing deeply. Finally, when I've got my errant body under control, I put away my overnight bag, nip to the loo and check the messages on my phone, then go down to join everyone for dinner.

Throughout the evening, I'm supremely conscious of every move Karima makes. It's as if there's nervous sensors along my body that can detect any change in hers. I'm finely attuned to her. I can tell, for instance, that she's not particularly keen on the mince pie she accepted on her plate a moment ago. Her face remains impassive as she bites into it and chews slowly, but it's obvious to me she doesn't like it. Dried fruit soaked in brandy is not to everyone's taste. She pauses, returning the pie to her plate, taking a breather from the arduous task of eating it. Quickly, before anyone notices, I grab it off her plate and pop it into my mouth. She turns to me in grateful surprise, and I give her a little wink.

Then, to take her mind off the matter, I ask about her work. She told us earlier about her promotion, and I'm curious about what it will entail. She begins to tell me about her ambitions for the overhaul of the English curriculum at her school. I question her thoroughly about her plans, genuinely interested in what she has to say. Actually, I'm blown away by the intelligence and lucidity of her thinking as she expounds on her ideas. I wonder if Karima realises just how extraordinary she is. I can't stop looking at her the rest of the evening. I try to be discreet, but she catches my glance a time or two, biting her lip nervously in response before looking quickly away. Hell, what am I doing?

Chapter 9

It's always been her

Next morning, I wake with a hard-on. No change then from how I went to bed. I've had visions of a naked Karima in my head on repeat, and for good measure, my active imagination has taken the scenario to the next level, with thoughts of her laid beneath me while I pump my raging cock into her.

With a groan, I take my hard shaft in hand and begin to stroke myself. Spreading the precum oozing out of my tip, I jerk rapidly on my cock, and it's not long before I come in great spurts that paint silver streaks on my abdomen. Damn. It's been a while since I've come like that. With a satisfied grunt, I heave myself upright and out of bed, then go shower. I dress in my old Christmas jumper that mum got me several years ago. It's tacky and cheesy, with a bright red reindeer on the front, but it's part of the occasion and I have no doubt everyone else will be in matching jumpers, even Karima. Ah yes, Karima, Allegra's best friend, my almost little sister who's been part of my family for years—and also now the star of my filthy dreams. If I don't rein in my dirty thoughts about her soon, it'll be obvious to everyone how I feel, and that would be damned awkward.

I just need to focus on not making an idiot of myself and not making Karima feel uncomfortable. It would be crazy to destroy the easy family dynamic we have, all over a sudden and intense, but surely passing attraction. After all, this can't go anywhere. My resolution is easier said than done. When Karima walks into the kitchen, my eyes jump to her, taking her in from head to toe and appreciating the swell of her breasts straining sensuously under the brightly coloured jumper she wears. She looks adorably cute decked out in red like a Christmas cracker, her dark hair swept into a loose knot at the back of her head, showcasing the graceful length of her neck. My cock thickens uncomfortably in the confines of my trousers as my eyes feast on her.

Rearranging myself discreetly, I see her come and sit on the stool beside me. I hide a smile as she struggles to perch herself on it. These things are not designed for anyone less than average in height. She's quiet then, sipping on her coffee and saying very little. I catch subtle notes of her scent and lean sideways, very slightly, to sniff a little more. Bad idea. All it does is increase my arousal. Shit. I need to get this situation under control.

I try to join in the conversation with everyone else, but my mind is troubled. What the fuck is happening to me? I've known Karima for years, and I've never reacted to her the way I'm doing now. All because I caught sight of what she looks like under the baggy clothes she likes to wear. How pathetic is that? I better get my mind out of the gutter and start acting like a normal, responsible, enlightened man of the twenty-first century. I need to stop objectifying the poor girl who has done nothing to deserve my lecherous desires. There and then I decide I will not let my gaze wander even an inch below her chin.

Karima laughs at something Allegra says, and my eyes, which had been fixed determinedly on my phone, fly up to her face, just in time to see her pearly white teeth bite into the softness of her bottom lip. And now, all I can think of is how much I'd like to sink my own teeth into those plush lips. Damn it all to hell! This is getting out of hand. I reach over for a slice of toast and butter it furiously, all the while chanting to myself, "Get a grip; get a grip."

A hand lands on my shoulder. It's mum. "Everything alright?" she asks softly, only for my ears.

I force a smile. "Yeah, just work stuff on my mind." It's not a total lie. My mind is going round in circles trying to resolve the quagmire that is the script for *Ruin*. "This latest project I'm working on is proving to be one giant headache," I tell her.

She pats my shoulder soothingly. "I'm sorry to hear it, darling, but can't you put it from your mind just for today?"

"I'll try," I say with a sigh, putting my phone away and taking a final gulp of my coffee.

After breakfast, and once presents have been unwrapped, we go for our customary walk along the Thames. Karima is unusually quiet while Allegra interrogates me about *Ruin*, and I tell her a little of the challenges I'm facing. Every so often, I cast a glance at Karima, but she looks to be deep in thought, her eyes staring blankly ahead. I wonder what's going on in her head. We reach the pub, and I volunteer to go get the drinks. When I get back to our table, I notice Allegra and Karima looking closely at something on her phone.

"What are you all looking at?" I ask curiously while setting out the drinks on the table.

Hugo answers, "We've just taken some photos of Karima for her online dating profile."

I purse my lips, fighting a grimace. I hate the idea, and I know I have absolutely no right to. If Karima wants to sign up for a dating website, then she's free to do so. Still, I don't like it. I don't like the idea of some asshole preying on her good nature or messing her about. Oh alright, I'll admit it. I don't like the idea of some asshole nibbling on those sweet lips or putting grabby hands on her lush body. So, sue me. I'm jealous. I know very well I have no right to be, no right at all, but logic and reason have gone out the door.

We get back to the house, and throughout the rest of the day, while we help prepare Christmas dinner then sit down to eat, I wrestle with myself, trying to work out why, after all these years, I'm suddenly so worked up about Karima. I join in the general conversation around me, but in my head, I'm peeling back layer after layer, trying to uncover the truth like I'm my own therapist. And what's becoming clear is that this didn't start yesterday, when she accidentally flashed me the goods. No, this has been building up for much longer, maybe since I took the decision over a year ago to move back to London—or even long before that.

For decades, I've put on a mask, played a part to fit in and get ahead. It's worked, sending me up into the stratosphere careerwise. It's helped me not feel so much of a fraud in this great mansion of a house, with a stepfather who talks nothing like the people I grew up alongside. Much as I care for Hugo and am grateful for all he's done for me, there is still a part of me that feels like I don't belong in his world. Inside, I'm still Wilfred O'Dowd from a council estate in Woolwich.

And now, I want... I want to let my guard down and be my authentic self with someone that gets me—the whole me. I want to be with someone with whom I can create the happy home I crave. It strikes me that maybe that person is right here in this room. I look across at Karima, and she intercepts my glance. For an eternal few seconds, we stare at each other before she looks shyly away.

Am I projecting? It's difficult to say. I have no clue what her feelings are, though I suspect she isn't indifferent to me. Everything about her speaks to that part of me that yearns for authenticity. And fuck, she turns me on too. But should I do something about it, or let sleeping dogs lie?

I still have no answer to that question when much later that afternoon, after we're all replete from our Christmas dinner, I bid everyone goodbye and head back to my house in Notting Hill. In between work calls and emails and script re-writes, I spend the next few days having a true reckoning with myself—that and having fevered dreams of Karima that don't seem to abate, not to mention jealous visions of her going out on a date with some nameless guy.

Slowly, painfully, I begin to drag the truth out of the closet. Gradually, I walk the path to admitting it, what I've been hiding from myself all this time. I've always had feelings for Karima. They may have been of a brotherly sort at first when she was still a child, but year by year they grew to something else. There's a reason I've always come home for the holidays and family birthdays, even when I lived abroad. Yes, it was to see my family, but it was also so I could see her. Her times of grief hit me hard. When I heard she lost her mum, I knew at once I wanted to reach out to her. She was young then, only fourteen, but my heart felt something of her pain, even then. I spent hours trying to find the right words to write to her.

Then it was her dad. She had already blossomed into an adult by then—an adult that had caught my eye and my heart. I debated what to do. I didn't have the guts then to act on my true wish, which was to go to her, wrap her in my arms and let her cry her pain in my embrace. Instead, I sent a text message, a bloody text. Then I spent the next day staring at my phone, willing a response. None came.

Of course not. What was I to her but some guy who happened to be her best friend's brother?

Over the next months and years, I gleaned what news of her I could through careful interrogation of Allegra. My heart leapt each time we met at family gatherings. But did I do anything about it? Fuck no. And here, the truth I've been avoiding is ugly. All those years, I was busy trying to make a name for myself, trying to prove that I wasn't Wilfred O'Dowd from a council estate but Wilfred Barton-Browne, a man going places, a man that belonged in the highest echelons of society. That man needed to have society girls and beautiful starlets on his arms. That man could not be seen to be in love with Karima, someone who quite obviously did not fit in that world he aspired to. So, subconsciously or not, I subsumed my feelings for her, plastered and papered over them. It's a bitter and unpalatable truth. Here I am, fearing that she'll meet some asshole online who'll take advantage of her, and all along it's me that's been the asshole.

It's not easy, coming to these realisations. I'm surly and angry with myself, but I don't wallow for too long. Work commitments pull me out of the negative spiral and force me to focus on matters other than myself. And perhaps there's also something of my bloody-minded spirit that cuts through the pity party. Yes, I have been a foolish bastard, but I can't change the past, only move forward. What I do know is that I have strong, unresolved feelings for a woman who probably views me as little more than an acquaintance, the brother of a friend. No, that's not quite true. Gut instinct tells me there *is* something more there, whether it's an unspoken chemistry or an affinity that is exerting a pull between us, it's something I can't ignore.

Nine thirty on New Year's Eve, at a glitzy party I had agreed to attend weeks ago, I'm surrounded by a thrum of glamorous people clamouring for attention, and I'm not feeling the vibe one bit. I love my work, love bringing movies to life, but this part of the lifestyle has gotten old very quickly. I see and hear the people around me like a blur. None of it feels real. It's almost as if I'm inside some movie scene, an audience watching us while munching on popcorn, and I'm about to break the fourth wall by tearing open the canvas of the screen and stepping out of the movie—reclaiming my freedom like Jim Carrey did in *The Truman Show* when he finally broke out of the film set he'd been living in. Nothing feels so right as the moment I make my excuses, to the surprise of those around me, and walk out of the party. I collect my coat and pull out my phone, hastily punching in the name of the person that's haunted my thoughts this past week and more. I'm not thinking through what I'll say. If I were thinking about it, I'd realise she's probably out somewhere with friends on this festive night. It doesn't matter. Like a lifeline leading me out of the fake world I'm breaking out of, her voice is what I need to hear right now.

Chapter 10

Please kiss me

My cab drops me off in front of Karima's house just before ten. I've never been here before, though the address is saved on my phone for the sending of Christmas and birthday cards. Ever since I took the decision to ditch the party and go see her, I've felt like a huge boulder has been removed from my shoulders. It's a sign, if ever I needed one, that finally, I'm doing the right thing. I don't know how things are going to shake down between me and Karima, and yet there's nowhere else I'd rather be this New Year's Eve.

I jump out of the cab and hurry to the front door, pressing on the bell. While I wait for it to open, I give the house a cursory glance. It's small and neat and unpretentious. Then my attention focuses on Karima, who stands at the door, smiling at me uncertainly. "Wilfred, hi," she says.

I hold out the bottle of Prosecco I procured on my way to her. She takes it from me and steps back to let me in. "You sure you don't mind me barging in on you like this?" I ask as I walk in.

"Of course not, come on in."

I follow her inside and close the door behind me. As soon as it shuts, I pull her to me for a hug, holding her a fraction longer than necessary. I take a deep inhale of her familiar scent—it's subtle, barely noticeable except to a connoisseur like me, an earthy aroma with a hint of spice. "Thanks for having me over," I say, a little gruffly.

"Thanks for coming and keeping me company," she retorts, taking my coat from me and hanging it on a peg in the small hallway. She leads me into the living room. It's cosy, furnished in warm tones of amber with touches of burgundy from the throw pillows. A bright rug over the wood floor adds another dash of colour to the room. Along one corner is a wide L-shaped couch, a soft blanket thrown casually over it. Across from it is a rustic-looking wooden coffee table on which sits a loaf-shaped cake on a platter, two small plates laid out beside it. A tall lamp in the opposite corner casts a warm yellowish hue over the room, completing the inviting, homey look.

"This is nice," I say, bending down to remove my shoes and leaving them in the hallway.

"Thanks," she says, pride evident in her voice. "I've only been here a few months, but it's home." She hovers by the door and asks hospitably, "Will you have some tea? I've got English Breakfast, Assam, Darjeeling and Roobois."

I shrug. "I don't mind, to be honest. Whatever you're having is fine with me."

She cocks her head to one side in thought. "How about Darjeeling? It'll go nicely with the cake."

"Darjeeling it is." She turns to walk out of the room, and I follow her to the small, square-shaped kitchen at the back of the house. It's immaculate, composed of matt dark blue units topped with a gleaming white worktop. I run my hand along its smooth edges, admiring the quality of the craftsmanship, a memory teasing at the edge of my mind. "Did your brother fit this?"

She looks surprised. "Yes, how did you know?"

"An educated guess. I remember you telling us about his work some years back. This looks really good, Karima."

She beams at me. "Thanks. I'm happy it turned out so well. Amir helped a lot, getting me a good wholesale deal on the units so I could splash out on something top of the range." She fills the kettle and switches it on, then reaches into a cupboard to take out the tea. I lean with my elbows on the counter, watching her as she potters about. This house, the kitchen, the warm and cosy living room, all of it carries her stamp. I love it. Presumptuous it might be, but I already feel right at home here.

She smiles again as she lays out two cups and saucers on a tray, together with a small jug of milk. "People talk of the old-boy network greasing the wheels of big business and politics, but it's not a patch on the networking in the building trade, if you ask me. Electricians, plumbers, tilers, decorators—you name it and my brother knows of someone he can call to do high quality work at the right price."

I chuckle. "I think it's like that in most trades. One of my film editors knows absolutely everyone in the movie trade—script writers, stunt co-ordinators, camerapeople, lighting and set designers—the works. Anytime I'm looking to put together a production team, he's the first person I ask about who's available and who would be a good fit for the job." I take the tray from her and carry it to the living room, depositing it on the coffee table.

"Speaking of the movie trade," she goes, pouring the tea into each cup, "how are things with *Ruin*?" I grimace and she prompts, "That bad?"

"I'm going to have to do something to break the deadlock soon," I say, "or else there won't be a movie project anymore." I watch her cut a slice of the cake and place it on a plate for me. "Thanks," I murmur, taking it from her. I plunge my fork into it and take a first bite. It's delicious, moist on the inside with a crumbly crust—nothing like the marble cakes one gets from the shops. I take another bite then wash it down with a warming gulp of tea. "This is so good," I moan pleasurably. My worries about the movie, my self-recriminations, my dissatisfaction with the social whirl around me—all that melts away as I lounge here with Karima in her cosy living room, drinking tea and eating cake. The simple pleasures of life are sometimes the most profound.

"Thank you, K," I tell her. "I needed this."

She pours me another cup of tea from the pot. "I'm glad to help," she says simply. "Now, the big question. What shall we watch?"

We end up choosing *Before Sunset*, a romantic indie film starring Ethan Hawke and Julie Delpy, which is a sequel to *Before Sunrise*, a movie that came out a few years ago to great acclaim. It's a low-budget affair that relies on the sparky dialogue between the two main protagonists, who met on a train and had a brief fling in the first movie. Here, they meet again, though their reunion is bittersweet.

We stretch out comfortably side by side on the couch, sharing the snug blanket. It's companiable and cosy. Occasionally, my thigh will touch hers and heat fills my loins, which are thankfully well covered by the blanket. It doesn't help that the nature of the drama we're watching is bringing out a romantic vibe to our evening, despite the platonic ground we're treading. The air is thick with unspoken need, both hers and mine. I'm almost sure of it. But I'll tread carefully, for now.

During an emotionally-charged moment in the movie, we exchange a long, heated look. I lean an inch towards her. She leans towards me. I'm not imagining it. She wants this. Then she bites her lip and turns back to the TV, the moment broken. *Don't jump the gun, Wilfred.* She's obviously not ready to take the plunge from friend to lover, and I have to respect that, frustrating though it is.

It's nearly midnight when the movie ends. "Let me get the Prosecco," mumbles Karima. I follow her to the kitchen, stuck to her side like superglue. I take the bottle and corkscrew from her while she gets out two champagne flutes, then we take them through to the living room. I pop the cork and pour the fizzing drink into each flute just in time as the clock strikes midnight.

"Happy New Year," I say, clinking her glass.

"Happy New Year," she replies, and we both take a sip, standing face to face. I set down my flute on the table and take hers, putting it on the table too.

"Come here," I say, opening my arms, with every intention of giving a friendly, affectionate hug. I enfold her in my embrace, holding her close as I nuzzle her hair. We sway together for several long moments, and with each second that we linger like this, we're both making our feelings clear. This is more than simply a familial embrace. This is anything but platonic. "Karima," I say huskily. She pulls back a fraction to look up at me, the need and desire evident in her eyes. "Will you let me kiss you?" She stares at me, then gives an infinitesimal nod, but that's not enough of a green light where I'm concerned. "Words, Karima," I admonish. "I need to hear your words."

"Yes," she whispers. "Please kiss me, Wilfred."

I place both palms to her cheeks and hold her face steady for my kiss, then staring deeply into her eyes, I lean down and touch my lips to hers.

Chapter 11

Let's do things right

Her lips are soft and gentle as they touch mine. We pull back then return for a second kiss, this time with parted lips. My tongue swipes into her mouth and locks with hers hungrily. I taste the Prosecco we've just drunk and the potently sweet flavour of Karima.

I tighten my embrace, slipping a hand through her hair to hold her in place as I deepen the kiss. Her soft, giving flesh feels so right under my touch. I feel her explore me in turn, running fingers over my bristly jaw, then tracing them up to the skin under my eyes and over my brow, as if she's mapping my face with her hands. It's unbelievably arousing to feel so wanted. Our kiss changes, becoming a little more languid as I take my time to nibble and explore, trailing my lips along her cheek, her jaw, nipping at her earlobe before tracing a path back to her mouth. I could do this all night. That gives me an idea.

In one swift movement, I swoop her into my arms and bring us down to the couch. She lets out a squeak of surprise as I laughingly settle her into my lap. "That's better," I breathe, nipping at her mouth. "Get comfortable, K. I plan on doing this for an awfully long time." And then I'm kissing her again, long and intimately, taking my time despite the needy hardness of my cock straining against the zipper of my trousers. I want her desperately, yet I also feel an urge to savour each moment and not rush things.

I don't know how long we make out on the couch. I have no concept of time as we lap at each other, nip, suck and gently kiss in succession. I drop hungry kisses all over her face, her eyelids, the tip of her nose, the sensitive crook of her neck. Everywhere I can, I explore with my lips, my tongue, my teeth. Just like Karima was doing earlier with her hands, I'm mapping her face with my touch, memorising every nook and cranny. It's not a one-way street either, as she's just as avid in her explorations, tracing a finger over the straight line of my brows, stroking the lobes of my ears, licking over my Adam's apple. And always, always, we come back to drink from each other's mouth, like a life-saving serum.

With every passing second, a certainty grows in my heart of the rightness of this. It's never been like this with anyone else before. And along with this certainty is a need to make sure I don't fuck this up by being too hasty and too greedy tonight. Whatever this thing is between us, it's precious and needs to be tended with care. My raging cock be damned.

Her lips are red and swollen by the time I finally tuck her face into the crook of my neck and snuggle her close. "It's late," I say. "I should probably head home."

"Stay."

Oh the temptation. I let out a long breath. "Much as I'd love to, it's best I go. Karima, I don't want to rush you into anything. This is all very new, and I don't want you to do anything you'll regret." I kiss her cheek one last time and gently push her off my lap so I can get to my feet.

"This is not the time to be gentlemanly," she says looking at me plaintively, all the while stifling a yawn. The poor thing can barely keep her eyes open.

I take her hands and pull her up to standing, then draw her into my arms. "Ok, so here's the plan," I say. "Tell me if you agree with it or not." I drop a kiss to the top of her head. "Let's do things properly. I haven't even taken you out on a proper date yet. How about I come back tomorrow, and we can spend the day together, then I'll take you out somewhere nice for dinner."

"So, this isn't just a one night thing?" she enquires, her face hidden in my chest.

I resist the urge to spank her bottom—only just. "You know better than that," I say softly.

Her dark eyes rise to meet mine. "Do I?"

I point between her and me. "What do think all this has been between us tonight? A casual hook-up with my sister's best friend? Did any of the past hour feel casual to you?"

She shakes her head. "No, but I haven't wanted to get my hopes up," she murmurs. "You do tend to leave a long line of casual girlfriends behind you."

I expel a frustrated sigh. "I suppose I walked into that one." I draw her to me once more and hold her tight, as if the action can make her believe what I know in my heart is true. This is different, nothing like the others. Then, I opt for something of the truth. "K, this thing between us didn't start tonight or even at Christmas, when you so adorably gave me an eyeful. It's been brewing for a lot longer than that. At least for me it has... Has it for you?"

Her snort is unamused. "The longest time," she mutters.

"So, maybe we've both been cowardly fools, hiding our feelings and not making a move. Or maybe the time just wasn't right. But I think now, it could be—a new year, a fresh start. Let's do things right."

"Ok," she breathes.

"Ok," I echo. "Come on, I'll walk you to your room and bid you goodnight." I see her cast a glance at the remains of our feast on the table. "Leave it to me," I say softly. "I'll tidy it up while I wait for my cab." Taking her hand in mine, I walk her up the stairs to her bedroom door, which she helpfully points out.

"Goodnight, Karima." I kiss her gently, being the gentleman I never knew myself to be. "This has been the best New Year's Eve ever."

"It has," she agrees. "Goodnight."

"I'll call you in the morning," I promise.

"Hmmm," she mumbles against my lips before turning to open the door. "Goodnight," she says shyly one last time, then shuts the door softly behind her. I stare at the closed door for a few moments, feeling stupidly dazed by tonight's events. Then, with a smile forming on my lips, I head down and take out my phone to call for a cab. I pick up the discarded plates, glasses and teacups, taking everything back to the kitchen, where I quickly stack them in the dishwasher. The champagne flutes, I wash by hand, not sure if they'll go in the dishwasher. I cover the remainder of the cake with cling film, which I find in one of the drawers, and wipe off stray crumbs from the counter until everything is spic and span. I hear some movement upstairs, the bathroom door opening and shutting, but she leaves me be. We've said our goodnights, after all. But I'll be back tomorrow. That's a promise. And I'm going to woo Karima Afzal until she realises that I'm the one, just as I'm certain already that she's the one for me.

PART THREE: TOGETHER

Chapter 12

And the award goes to...

Karima, 18 years previously

What a surreal experience tonight has been. It's not my first time on the red carpet with Wilfred, as I accompanied him to the world and UK premieres of *Ruin*. But this bash tonight takes the cake. Talk about a lot of people dressed up to the nines in over-the-top designer clothes and dripping diamonds like there's no tomorrow.

Cameras are flashing constantly. People stop by to say hello and pose. Microphones are thrust into people's faces and rapid-fire questions asked, the networks hungry for a good soundbite for their TV broadcasts. And in the midst of all this there's me, clutching tightly to Wilfred's hand. He's promised, bless him, to stay close all evening and not abandon me to the wolves. Nobody is paying much attention to me, thankfully. All the focus is on him. My handsome, clever husband who's produced the movie nobody thought could be made. Not everyone can appreciate just how tough the process has been, but I've had a bird's-eye view of the whole, painful gestation of this amazing movie. It makes me all the more proud of him tonight because I know just how hard he's worked to make this happen.

He's looking amazing in his made-to-measure tux which fits his admittedly very fit body like a glove. Did I say I was proud? I am, and very smug, God forgive me. Because, ladies, models and glamorous movie stars here tonight, tall and toned and beautiful you might be, but he's all mine. And to be fair, I've not scrubbed up too badly either. I had a stylist come over weeks ago who helped me pick just the right dress to flatter my figure and complexion. My hair and make-up was done professionally, and I'm wearing the gorgeous earrings Wilfred gifted me for my thirtieth birthday. If I say so myself, I don't look too bad. It's amazing what a well-cut dress and good styling can do. And that's saying something, considering I'm still trying to get my figure back after giving birth to our daughter, Layla, four months ago. I've lost most of the weight, but there's no doubt flesh is rather wobbly around the middle. No problem though. This miracle of a dress has some sort of inbuilt corset that gives me definition. The look on Wilfred's face when he first set eyes on me earlier tonight? Priceless. It's a memory I'm not likely to forget in a hurry.

"Fuck, you're gorgeous," he'd said. I felt like Cinderella—only there's no pumpkin at midnight, because this wonderful fantasy is real.

Our courtship has been something of a whirlwind. After that first smooch on New Year's Eve, we went out on several dates, but it wasn't long before we ended up in bed. To be fair, I was a sure thing from day one, but Wilfred wanted to be the gentleman and to woo me properly. God, that man is sweet. He popped the question on Valentine's Day, six weeks into our courtship. We both knew that this was it. We had no doubts, so why wait? As Harry most memorably said to Sally, when you realise you want to spend the rest of your life with somebody, you want the rest of your life to start as soon as possible.

And married life so far? It's been great. Ok, so there have been some adjustments. It takes work to mesh two lives together, especially with lifestyles as different as ours. And yet it hasn't been so very difficult, mostly because, underneath the veneer of it all, we're both a lot more similar than people realise, and we both want the same thing from our relationship. We're on the same page, so to speak. I've been good for Wilfred, grounding him in real life when the glitz and fakery of Hollywood threatens to overwhelm him. I'm his backbone, his sounding board and his support system all in one. And he does the same for me. Under his cheerleading, I've been encouraged to apply for an assistant head position at my school. And miracle of miracles, I got it. I've taken a leaf or two out of his book and learned to have the courage of my convictions and to stop second guessing myself all the time. I'm good at what I do, so why shouldn't I get promoted? Yay for me.

And now we're sat in the auditorium while the Oscars are given out, category by category. *Ruin* won the best adapted screenplay, but missed out narrowly on the best director. Finally, the moment we've all been waiting for has arrived: the best film award. Snippets from each movie are played for the audience, then it's time to make the announcement. I feel Wilfred tense beside me. I squeeze his hand under the table. God, the anticipation is painful. Can we get this over with?

"And the Oscar goes to... *Ruin!*"

A big cheer goes up from the cast and crew sitting around us. Wilfred's eyes meet mine, and for a brief second, there's a vulnerable look on his face—he's Wilfred O'Dowd from a council estate in Woolwich, wondering if it really is him people are cheering or whether everyone's found him out as an impostor. I hold his stare reassuringly, then throw my arms around him. "You did it," I murmur into his ear. "You did it." His grip around me tightens, but he's too emotional to speak. "Go on," I whisper. "Go get your gong." With a nod and a final smouldering look at me, he makes his way to the stage while the audience, me included, claps and cheers.

I watch proudly, and a little tearfully, as he accepts the Oscar and begins his acceptance speech. There's a whole list of people he has to thank, and then, he clears his throat and his eyes find me in the audience. "Many people thought I was mad to embark on this project. How on earth can a story like *Ruin* be told in a movie? And yes, I'll admit, it was a crazy idea. Some days, it felt like an impossible task. But I had this vision which I clung to, even in the darkest days. And I've also been incredibly lucky, because when it got tough—and it got tough a lot of times—I had one person cheering me on and telling me not to quit. That person is my lovely wife, Karima. So really, this award is hers, just as much as it is mine. Thank you, K. Love you so much."

Now my tears are in full flow, smudging my mascara. Someone helpfully hands me a tissue, and I hastily try to repair the damage. Then Wilfred is back, and I'm in his arms again. He holds me close as he whispers, over and over, "I love you, love you, love you." Oh my heart. It feels like it could explode.

"Love you too," I manage, then tear myself away so we can sit down and regain our composure. All around him, there's lots of back thumping and congratulatory words. It's dizzying. I feel his hand creep under the table to grab mine and hold on. He doesn't let go all evening. Not until we're in the limo, heading to the hotel. In the quiet stillness of the car, he draws me to his side and leans his head backwards, closing his eyes in contented relief. I breathe deeply and relax into his body. What a night! Now, it's back to real life.

No sooner does the thought cross my mind than my phone begins to buzz loudly. I extract if from the minuscule handbag it's in and answer. "Allegra," I say, and Wilfred sits up beside me. I put the phone on speaker so he can hear.

"Ok, so great news about the Oscar, but any chance you can get here soon?" she demands, sounding more than a little harried.

"We're five minutes away from the hotel," responds Wilfred. "What's wrong?"

"I've changed her, fed her, rocked her. I've even sung her a damned lullaby, but she won't stop crying. Please help."

Wilfred's eyes fly to mine in pained amusement. Yeah, we've been here before. "Keep rocking her gently," I say, "and stroke a hand down her tummy. She likes that. We'll be there soon, so you won't have to hold the fort for much longer."

"Ok," she huffs. "Be quick."

I end the call and return the phone to my clutch bag. Wilfred chuckles quietly beside me. "Well, if that isn't a drop back down to earth."

"I was just thinking the very same thing," I say.

He laughs and pulls me in for a kiss. "Wouldn't have it any other way."

Neither would I.

Chapter 13

◆ ── ♥ ── ➤

A delightful surprise

Present day

The day went by quickly, as it always did in the fast-paced world of school. She had a brief moment to check her phone at lunchtime, but there was nothing from Wilfred. No surprise—it was still the early hours of the morning in LA. On the plus side, there was a sweet message from her daughter, who was currently teaching English in France on her gap year.

Karima wolfed down her sandwich, then it was time to go to the playground for her stint on duty, after which there was no further opportunity to check her phone. Finally, at a quarter to five, she packed her things and prepared to leave for the day, wishing everyone a happy half-term. Relief in every step, she made her way to the car, glad to have the next week off so she could re-charge. Sometimes, this job took every ounce of her energy.

As she strapped her seatbelt on, her phone buzzed with an incoming message.

Wilfred: Happy Valentine's Day sweet girl. You still at work?

Karima: About to head home. Happy Valentine's Day to you too, gorgeous.

Wilfred: Drive safe and call me when you get home. I've missed you.

Karima: Missed you too. Speak soon xxxxx

She put the phone down, her heart several degrees lighter. She had known, of course, that Wilfred wouldn't forget. She had no doubts of his affection or of her place in his life. This morning's glumness had merely been a manifestation of her missing him. She hated their separations. Hopefully, these would be fewer in the years to come.

Pulling out of her parking space, she began the trafficky drive back home, putting on a romantic audiobook to listen to on the journey. Some forty minutes later, she pulled into the drive of the large detached house they had bought in west London shortly after their marriage. Bag in hand, she slammed the car door and hurried up the front steps to the house, letting herself in with the key. The alarm was off, so Hamid must already be home from school. "I'm home!" she called, removing her coat and hanging it on a peg in the hallway. She dropped her bag on the side table, toed off her shoes and stepped into her waiting slippers. Ah, that felt much better.

With a spring in her step, she headed to the kitchen to put the kettle on before calling Wilfred in LA—and came to an abrupt halt. A naked man, save for the tiny apron he wore, was busy chopping up vegetables at the kitchen counter. The round globes of his arse peeked cheekily at her from under the back ties of the apron. She would know that arse anywhere.

"Wilfred!"

He turned to her with a grin. "Ta-dah!"

She continued to stand in place, astonishment rendering her motionless for a brief moment. It gave him time to put the knife and chopping board safely out of harm's way before she launched herself at him. He caught her in his strong arms and held her tight as she cried, "You're back!"

"I'm back," he said, kissing the top of her head. They stayed clutched together for several, emotionally-charged seconds.

"You really threw me off the scent with that text," she murmured, drawing back a fraction to look at him. "I was all set to call you in LA."

"I know," he replied. "Didn't want to give the game away too soon."

She touched her palms to his smooth cheeks. Evidently, he had showered and shaved on his arrival in the UK. "Not that I'm complaining, but how come you're back so soon?" she wondered.

"Remember that out of body experience I had at that New Year's Eve party before I came to see you all those years ago?"

She nodded. He had told her about how he had felt weirdly detached from all the goings on around him, and walked out on the glitz and glamour to give her that fateful call.

"Well," he said, dropping a kiss on the tip of her nose, "it happened again. I was in a ghastly meeting, words being volleyed back and forth, and after a while, it became this garbled noise in my ears. All I could think of was you, alone in our bed when I should have been with you."

"So, you walked out on the meeting?" She eyed him incredulously.

He smirked. "I knocked some heads together, then walked out, leaving Irene in charge."

A laugh spluttered out of her. "That must have gone down well."

He snorted, "As well as could be expected." Then he kissed his wife again. "It'll sort itself out, but right now, I don't give a toss about any of it. I want to be with you." He dropped his arms from around her and stepped back, twirling around to give her a show. "What do you think of this outfit?"

"I think it might catch on as the newest trend," she told him, straight faced.

He looked down at himself. "Still rocking it for a fifty-six year old?"

His belly had softened with age, and there were greys in the hairs on his chest, but he was still the most handsome man she knew. "You know you still do it for me," she confirmed. Casting a glance at the kitchen counter, she went on, "In fact, I have a question for you, my love. Well, two questions. First, where's Hamid, and second, will that lovely dinner spoil if we leave this kitchen for twenty minutes?"

He dropped an arm around her shoulder and drew her to him. "Your son was expensive to bribe, K. I saw him when he got back from school and had a word. He's staying over at Amir's tonight."

She frowned. "What has he asked for?"

Wilfred merely shook his head. "We'll talk about that another time. As for the food, it's all good for the time we need. I only put the lasagna in the oven a minute ago." He glanced slyly at his wife. "Upstairs or on the living room rug?"

Karima was already leading him out of the kitchen. "The living room, seeing as we have the house to ourselves."

"Right answer," he said approvingly.

A few quick strides brought them to the living room, the curtains already drawn and a cheery fire burning in the hearth. It was toasty warm in here, just right for what they had in mind. With careful deliberation, Wilfred untied the apron and pulled it off, throwing it over the nearest sofa.

He stood on display for her, hands at his sides, and said with a lift of his brow, "Your turn."

There was no shyness to be had where he was concerned. Wilfred knew every inch and contour of her body, and showed his appreciation on a daily basis. She was still not very sylph-like. In fact, there were at least several pounds of flesh more on her body now than there had been twenty years ago. Who cared? Not them.

She slipped her socks and slacks off first, then the soft woollen sweater she wore. This left her in the simple cotton pants she liked to wear—comfort came first in her book—and a plain white bra that gave her boobs the right support without digging into her flesh. Wilfred had no complaints. He watched her with greedy, lust-filled eyes. Under his warm gaze, she made short work of the rest of her clothes, coming to stand naked before him.

"Do that thing I like," he growled.

He didn't need to explain. It was his little fetish, ever since that Christmas Eve two decades ago when he had walked in on her and caught her in the buff. With a knowing smile, she turned sideways to show him her profile, then grasped both breasts, filling her hands with the soft flesh and lifting slightly before letting them fall away with a delightful bounce.

A rumble came from his chest. "Again," he demanded. She complied.

"Still do it for you?" she enquired.

"Oh yes," he vowed, then he pounced.

Karima's Marble Cake

Ingredients:

1 3/4 cups plain (all purpose) flour

1 1/2 tsp baking powder

1/2 tsp salt

1/2 cup sunflower oil (or any other neutral oil)

1 1/4 cups sugar

4 eggs

1 tsp vanilla extract

1/2 cup milk

For the chocolate batter:

3 tbsp cocoa

2 tbsp milk

Instructions:

Preheat oven to 180°C (350°F). Grease and line a non-stick loaf tin (9 x 5 inches).

Combine the flour, baking powder and salt in a small bowl, whisk to remove lumps, and set aside.

In a large mixing bowl, mix the oil, sugar, eggs and vanilla on high speed with an electric whisk for about two minutes until mixture is a creamy yellow batter.

Alternate adding the flour and milk to the batter in small batches, using a wooden spoon or hand whisk to gently combine without overmixing.

Take out about a cup of the batter and place it in a separate bowl, adding the 3 tbsp of cocoa and 2 tbsp milk and mixing gently to create the chocolate batter.

Alternate pouring the vanilla and chocolate batters into the lined loaf tin to create a swirly effect. You can also use a knife to swirl the batter together to get it "marbly".

Bake in the lower shelf of the oven for an hour or until it's toothpick clean. Wait for it to cool before you enjoy - if you can!

Afterword

Happy Valentine's Day, dear reader, wherever you are and whoever you're with (or not). I hope you enjoyed this heartwarming little story of two people's journey of love. If you would like to read another Valentines novella of mine, this one quite a bit spicier, then do grab yourself a copy of **My Secret Affair with the Trillionnaire**.

Please do also consider subscribing to my newsletter on **mmwakeford.substack.com** to get latest authorly news, book recommendations and freebies, or check out my website, **mw-author.com**, for more in-depth information about my publications.

May I ask you for a small favour?

Reviews are the life blood of independent authors. Please could you help spread the word about this book by submitting a review on **Amazon, Goodreads** or any other book reader platform. Thank you!

M.M. Wakeford

About the author

M.M. Wakeford lives with her husband and son in a London terraced house that gathers dust while she loses herself in her writing. A lifelong reader of romantic novels, she writes in many genres including contemporary, sci-fi and historical romance.

Her stories capture that heady feeling of falling in love, with emotionally rich characters whose journey to a happily ever after is lined with dilemmas, desire and difficult choices. If you're looking for a page turning romance with high emotion and a good dose of spice, you're in the right place.

To be the first to hear about new releases, sneak previews and exclusive extras, sign up for M.M. Wakeford's mailing list at <u>mw-author.com</u>.

Also by this author

MY SECRET AFFAIR WITH THE TRILLIONAIRE

In a glittering future where pleasure and power collide...

I never meant to fall for a client.

As a Master Healer, I offer therapeutic touch that ends in release—professional, intimate, perfectly legal. It pays well. It's flexible. And it lets me give my daughter the life she deserves.

Every Friday at six, Tobias Moore walks through my door.

Yes, *that* Tobias Moore—trillionaire, media darling, devastatingly untouchable. He never speaks more than necessary. Never lingers. And never, ever breaks the rules.

Until the day I accidentally reveal what I've been hiding: I want him just as badly as my hands suggest.

The next session, everything changes.

"I'm not one to beat about the bush, Viva. I want you."

His offer is simple: a secret affair. No media. No strings. Just stolen moments in the shadows of his impossible life.

I should say no. Getting involved with someone like Tobias could shatter everything I've built. But when desire this intense is finally within reach... how can I possibly walk away?

A high-heat futuristic romance about forbidden desire, secret affairs, and risking it all for a love that was never supposed to happen.

MY CAPTIVE DUCHESS
Book 1 – The Reeves of Reeves Hall

"You cannot leave Reeves Hall again. Here you will remain."

Recently widowed, Jane, Duchess of Coleford, has retreated to a remote estate in Cornwall with her young daughter. There she meets her formidable neighbour, Brook Reeves — a man with a permanent scowl and a stubborn streak to match her own. He wants her gone, making repeated offers to buy the crumbling house she inherited from her late husband. Jane refuses, determined to stay... and not admit how much she is drawn to him.

But one day, Jane ventures uninvited into his domain and discovers secrets she must never reveal. There is only one solution: at Reeves Hall, she must remain — his captive duchess.

What you'll find inside:
- ♥ Forced proximity romance
- ♥ Enemies-to-lovers tension
- ♥ Grumpy/sunshine main characters

♥ Mr Rochester/Jane Eyre vibes

♥ Slow-burn but steamy

♥ Regency romance with a sci-fi twist

My Captive Duchess is Book 1 in *The Reeves of Reeves Hall* series, featuring the mysterious Reeves family. Each book can be enjoyed as a standalone, with its own hero, heroine, and happily ever after. If you love page-turning, heart-stopping romance with an original, genre-blending twist, this story is for you.

Praise for My Captive Duchess:

"Absolutely outstanding writing... Original story with uncompromising storytelling that you will have difficulty putting down once you start reading." ★★★★★ Goodreads review

"A seamless blend between the two genres, throw in some spice, a strong & feisty FMC, a cute daughter, and a stubborn manly-man with the weight of balancing two worlds, and you have a winner... exceptional writing and story-telling." ★★★★★ Goodreads review

"The most fascinating story I have read in a long while... a wonderful read!" ★★★★★ Goodreads review

"I found the story so engaging I couldn't put it down." ★★★★★ Goodreads review

"I applaud the clever plot in this story. I adore both Regency and Sci-Fi, but never expected to see a combination of my two favorites! Well done!" ★★★★★ Goodreads review

SERIES BY M. M. WAKEFORD

THE REEVES OF REEVES HALL
Steamy Regency Romance With a Dash of Sci-fi

Book 1 - MY CAPTIVE DUCHESS
Book 2 - MY MASQUERADE WITH THE DUKE
Book 3 - A NOT SO CONVENIENT MARRIAGE

THE STANTON LEGACY
High Spice Historical Romance

Book 1 - THE VISCOUNT'S SCANDALOUS AFFAIR
Book 2 - THE VIXEN'S UNLIKELY MARRIAGE
Book 3 - THE BLUESTOCKING'S SECRET OBSESSION
Book 4 - THE VISCOUNT'S FORBIDDEN LOVE
Book 5 - MISS STANTON MEETS HER MATCH
Book 6 - MR TEMPLETON FINDS HIMSELF A WIFE

THE VENORIANS AND KROVATIANS
High Spice Sci-fi Romance

Book 1 - KRANTOR'S MATE
Book 2 - MELINDA'S CHOICE
Book 3 - LAIJAR'S TEMPTATION

LOVE AGAINST THE ODDS
High Spice Contemporary Romance

Book 1 - LIBERATION
Book 2 - DUPLICATION
Book 3 - DETERMINATION

SEASONAL NOVELLAS
Standalone quick reads with swoony heroes & happily
ever afters

IT'S ALWAYS BEEN YOU
MY SECRET AFFAIR WITH THE TRILLIONAIRE

*For more information about M.M. Wakeford's
publications, please visit* **mw-author.com**.